I am not
most places

I am not most places

stories by
Richard Cumyn

A Porcépic Book
an imprint of Beach Holme Publishing Limited

This edition published by Beach Holme Publishers, #226--2040 West
12th Ave., Vancouver, BC, V6J 2G2, with the assistance of The
Canada Council and the BC Ministry of Small Business, Tourism and
Culture. This is a Porcépic Book.

This is a work of fiction. Names, characters, places, and incidents
are the product of the author's imagination or are used fictitiously,
and any resemblance to actual persons, living or dead, events or
locales is entirely coincidental.

Editor: Joy Gugeler
Cover and Interior Photos of Slocan Park, BC: Antonia Banyard
Production and Design: Antonia Banyard

Canadian Cataloguing in Publication Data:

Cumyn, Richard, 1957-
    I am not most places

"A Porcépic Book."
ISBN 0-88878-373-6

I. Title.
PS8555.U4894I12 1996   C813'.54C96-910546-0
PR9199.3.C776I12 1996

Author's Note

I am grateful to the following publications, in which some of these stories first appeared in different form:

The New Quarterly: "Reconfigured" (as "Rosalyn Road"); *The Blue Penny Quarterly*: "Perennial" (as "I Am Not Most Places") and "Home Free"; *Acta Victoriana*: "Sarasota"; *Swiftsure*: "From Where I Live Now"; *The Canadian Forum*: "Someone You Can Count On" and *The NeWest Review*: "Day of Reckoning".

Acknowledgements

For their help with indidvidual stories, I thank Alan and Steven Cumyn, Ian Colford, Thomas Hubschman, and Steven Heighton; for her uncompromising vision, I am indebted to my editor, Joy Gugeler; but for the love and encouragement of my wife, Sharon Murphy, this book would not have been made.

For Vivien and Elizbeth,
heart-warmers and veterans of the move

Contents

heat stroke

Rather than take the car into the underground garage, Bill parked in one of the spots reserved for visitors. He left his clubs in the trunk. Leona was sitting on the grass in the shade beside the front doors, rocking back and forth and humming to herself. The baby was asleep. Doreen was pushing the carriage away from her and pulling it back. He asked her what was going on. The sun had burnt a wide ring around the back of her neck and on the top of her shoulders where they were exposed. The baby's clothes were soaked through.

"We should go inside now," he said. Doreen did not respond, only rocked the pram with one hand and chewed the nails of the other.

"I'm going to take the kids inside now, Doreen. Are you coming? What are you looking at?"

"She'll be back any minute."

"Who? Who will be back?"

"I can't just leave her."

"Who are you talking about? Come inside with me."

"I can't. Not yet. You take the children in."

He spoke angrily. She seemed to slide inside herself. He

had to pry her fingers off the handle of the carriage – how long had she been gripping it with such force? Had she been standing there like this all day?

He brought the children inside. The baby sucked down a whole bottle of milk and then another of water. Leona found something to watch on television. Bill regretted what he had said to Doreen, but he couldn't understand. What kind of mother would keep her children outside in the cruel sun all day?

Leona ate a bowl of cereal for supper and fell asleep at the table. He carried her to her room and put her in bed still in her clothes. Kenny refused to lie in his crib. Bill paced the living room, rocking him. Periodically the baby brought his knees up to his chest and howled. Bill walked with him high against his shoulder, singing an old song that had once soothed him, but Kenny wasn't having any of it. Bill got a blanket to cover him, brought him down in the elevator, and stepped outside.

The air was cooler now and the light fading. They walked over to the corner where Doreen had been, turned left down Vine and then headed up one of the streets that coiled upon itself like a snake devouring its tail. He looked back and could no longer see their building. The baby dozed against his shoulder.

Bill stopped walking when he saw Doreen come out of a doorway, cross the lawn and ring the doorbell of the next house. The door opened and she said something at length to the man who answered. He was fat and wore only an undershirt and boxer shorts. The man shook his head. Doreen turned her shoulders, nodded, and they exchanged a final word. She walked towards the street, the man watching her for a moment. He saw Bill looking, and quickly closed his door.

Bill called to her. She walked up the empty street to where he was standing.

"Where's Leona? You shouldn't have left her."

"She went right to sleep. I wanted to see how you were. I was worried."

"Don't be."

She looked away. Finally he said, "Are you coming home now?"

"This isn't going to take me long."

"What isn't? What's not going to take you long?"

She could see he was not going to leave without an explanation.

* * *

She had been sketching in the park earlier in the morning. When she looked up from her drawing, a little girl was staring at her. Slowly the child moved around the monkey bars until she was standing beside the bench where Doreen was sitting.

Doreen said, "Hello, what's your name?"

"I'm not supposed to talk to strangers."

Leona ran over to her. "We're not strangers," she said, "you're the stranger."

"Leona, I think the little girl would prefer to be alone. You go back to your swing. Mind you don't wake Kenny." Doreen returned to her drawing.

"My mother told me I should go out and play and never come back."

"She didn't. I think you're telling stories," said Doreen without looking up from her sketching surface, a piece of particle board laid across her lap. The child crawled between her feet and curled up under the board.

"What are you doing down there?" Doreen said with a startled laugh. She uncrossed her legs and lifted the board to look. The child wormed beneath her long skirt until her head rested on Doreen's lap.

"Come out of there," said Leona, who had returned to rescue her mother. She seized the child roughly by the arm and yanked. The child tumbled onto her side at Doreen's feet, brought her knees to her chest, jammed her thumb into her mouth, and slid her other hand under the waistband of her shorts. When Doreen tried to pull her into a sitting position, the child shrieked.

"Do you know where her mother is?" Doreen asked a woman who had been attracted by the commotion.

"No, I thought she was yours."

They took turns trying to get the child to talk, asking her name, her address, the name of her school, her favourite toys, what she liked to watch on television, whether or not she had brothers and sisters. This continued until the other woman excused herself, calling her son down from an elm.

Kenny roused from sleep in his pram and began to cry. The girl whimpered, as if in chorus. Leona whined to be taken home.

"We can't just leave her here."

"Can she come home with us?" Leona asked.

"I suppose she'll have to." Doreen's morning collapsed before her eyes into stringy clots of red.

"We have to go now," she said, bending closer to the child. When Doreen tried to pick her up, the girl recoiled and screamed as if burnt.

"I don't want to leave you here, but if you don't come with us now, you'll be all alone." She felt an odd urge to append terror to the promise of solitude.

"I want to be alone."

"Fine. Good-bye. Come on, Leona."

Doreen began to walk away, slowly, expecting the child to call out, to run after her, at least to pick herself up. She stopped pushing Kenny's carriage, bent over to adjust his soother, and glanced back at the child. She would have to call the police.

When she returned with the officers, the girl was gone. The team, a man and a woman, began to ask Doreen questions. What were her feelings about disciplining children? Did she ever resent her daughter and son? What time of day did she find the most depressing? Doreen tried to answer each question dispassionately. She said she had called out of a feeling of desperation.

"She crawled up between my legs and hid her head beneath my skirt. Think of it – for God's sake!"

"Ma'am, you didn't tell us that before," but Doreen insisted that she had.

6

"Leona, tell the officers what you saw."

Leona clung to Doreen's skirts and sucked her thumb. She shook her head "No" to everything the officers asked her. Had she seen a little girl who was alone in the park? Had Leona's mother seen a little girl? Was Leona telling a lie? Did Leona's mother ever spank her for being bad?

"Now wait just a minute!"

The man put up his hand. "Clearly your daughter has no recollection of the event. Was she nearby at the time?"

"She was right beside me. You've made her afraid to speak."

The woman, feeling Doreen's distress, redirected. "Ma'am, she's probably back home by now. We've had no report of a missing child in the vicinity. We have your statement, your description of her. There's nothing else we can do. Would you like us to drive you home?"

Doreen declined coolly and began to push Kenny's carriage, with Leona alternately lagging behind and sprinting ahead. The police walked back to the cruiser.

A block away from the next intersection, Doreen saw the girl sitting on the front step of a townhouse.

"So this is where you live."

"No, it's not. I don't know where I live. I can't find my house."

"You're a little liar. This is your house. Go on inside," said Doreen. She took hold of the child by the upper arm and pulled her to her feet.

"Let go of me, you're hurting me. This isn't where I live. I swear. I don't know which house is mine."

"We'll see about that," said Doreen as she pressed the door-bell. They waited. She rang again. No answer. She tried the door, but it was locked.

"I don't think this is where she lives, Mum. I've seen other kids go in here."

"Just be quiet and let me think." Turning to the girl, arm still gripped tightly, she said, "If you don't tell me your name, I'm going to let go of you and walk away. I have my own children to take care of. I'm not playing any more games. You tell me everything you can remember about your mother and father and brothers and sisters, if you have any. Do you hear what I'm saying?" The girl nodded. "Leona knows her full name, address and telephone number, don't you, Leona?"

Leona recited the information, proud of her recall and speed.

"Now, can you do what Leona did?"

The girl began to sob again.

"I can't, I can't," she shuddered.

"Your name. You have to have a name."

"Stupid. That's my name. My name is Stupid."

Doreen saw the child's pathetic life all in one flash. She moved her hand to the girl's shoulder and pressed a tentative hug. The girl flung her arms around Doreen's waist and buried her face in her middle.

"It's all right. You don't have to worry now. You come home with us. We'll get to the bottom of this," Doreen said, feeling the soup of rage and tenderness settle deep inside. She took the small hand gently in her own.

Leona immediately ran and grabbed Doreen's other hand, leaving her unable to push the carriage. She told Leona to help by taking hold of the girl's other hand. They progressed that way, spread across the concrete sidewalk.

The strange child's face brightened. She let go of Doreen's hand and joined Leona, hopping, skipping, singing, the two of them bounding ahead.

"Stop at the corner, you two."

They were laughing now, the girl's face alight with mischief as they approached the intersection. She nudged Leona to cross with her, to go ahead without Doreen. Leona, still laughing, resisted politely. They were four houses ahead of Doreen now. She quickened her pace and tried to steady the carriage as it bumped across the uneven joints of the sidewalk.

"Just wait 'til I get there."

The girl pulled hard at Leona. Doreen called for them to

stop, but they were already into the road. Leona followed the girl into the middle of the street and froze. A car turning quickly off Montpelier squealed its tires. The car skidded to a stop, its bumper just kissing Leona's thigh as she rotated away from it.

Doreen's scream blended with the sound of the tires and a second driver's horn. She ran out into the snarl of cars, picked Leona up in her arms, and raced to the opposite side.

The driver called out his window, "Is she hurt? Should I wait for the police?"

"No, she's all right," said Doreen, and waved him on. She crossed the intersection again, Leona riding her hip. Doreen grabbed the carriage with her free hand, waited for the traffic to break, and maneuvered her children across.

"Don't you ever! Don't you ever!"

"I won't, Mommy. I'm sorry. She was pulling me."

"Where did she go now? Where is the little...?" she said gazing about her, just paces from the entrance to her own building. "Where is she?" Doreen fumed.

Kenny began to cry for his afternoon bottle. Doreen, without a watch, tried to estimate how much time had passed. It might have been an hour, maybe three or four. The midsummer sun was still high, but that meant nothing.

"I'm thirsty," said Leona, pulling at her to go inside. Doreen was not thirsty or hungry. She felt abraded, entire layers of her skin missing.

She rolled the carriage back and forth to soothe Kenny. He can wait, she thought.

"Stop whining, Leona. We'll go inside in a minute. There's something Mommy has to see to."

She gave Kenny his soother. He fussed, fell asleep, awoke, wailed, worked the soother with his tongue. At seven Bill came home and found them standing on the corner in front of their building.

* * *

"It's late to be ringing people's doorbells," said Bill. "Besides, you can't haul her out of her own home."

"I wish you could have seen her," she sighed.

They didn't talk as they walked back. Towards Vine Street, Doreen gripped Bill's arm. The girl came skipping towards them. As she neared them, she changed her gait to a walk.

"Hello again," she said to Doreen. "It's getting late. I'm going home now. My mother's worried sick about me."

Doreen's mouth dropped and she stiffened.

"You show me where you live. Go ahead."

"Well, I'm really not supposed to talk to strangers. You can watch me go in, I guess. I can't stop you from watching, but I can't tell you my name."

"Just do it. Just go up to any one of these houses and go in. Show me."

She skipped up the street, and Doreen hurried after her, retracing her steps along the long curve. Bill followed with Kenny. The girl stopped in front of the house where Doreen had called earlier. "This is my house here," she announced.

"Good," said Doreen. "You just go on in, then."

"All right, I will. You don't believe this is my house, do you?"

"You're right, I don't."

The child's face twitched as if she were about to cry, but she recovered quickly. She smiled directly at Doreen. "Too bad for you." She marched up to the front door and pressed the door bell. The fat man, still in his underwear, opened the door and listened as the girl spoke to him. He scowled past her to where Doreen and Bill were standing. He ushered the child inside and promptly closed the door.

"That's not where she lives, it can't be," said Doreen, already moving up the walk. She knocked loudly on the door with her fist.

"Doreen."

Bill's voice roused Kenny, who began to cry. The man opened the door.

"I know she doesn't live here," said Doreen above Kenny's escalating cry. "I want her to come home with me."

The man pulled his door shut. The outside light went out. Doreen continued to pound on the door.

"I don't know what she's told you, but you shouldn't trust her. I want you to let her come home with me."

All the lights inside the house went out and the living room curtains were yanked closed.

"He's covering for her, Bill. Why is he doing it? I hate this place. Why did we have to move here, anyway? Why did you make me come?"

"It's not the place, it's the heat," he said.

"What did you say?"

"This is as good a place as any."

reconfigured

Barry Carp admitted that he had stumbled into the rental business the way he had most endeavours in his life.

"Friend of mine, guy I did time with, saw this place going for the second mortgage, cheap, so we went in on her together. You should have seen her back then. Hooo-boy."

"Not great?" said Peter.

"The worst. Not fit for habitation, man. Lot of hours went into this baby."

"So, you were in jail?"

"Two years. You don't want to hear about it. Let's just say I got a temper, especially 'round women. My wife'll attest to that. Man, it's a wonder she sticks it out. We got a kid, little girl, about a year younger than yours. Everything's under control. Now Colette, she's a looker. You figured her out yet?"

Peter's laugh came out short and flat.

"When you figure her out, you come and tell me," said Barry. "Hardest thing I know is understanding women. It baffles me. Flat out baffles."

* * *

"The man is a pig," said Colette. "He comes into our home, always at mealtime I'm sure you've noticed, unannounced, and proceeds to foul up the kitchen with his language and smoke. I'm fed up. Think of the baby. Sean is at a very formative stage right now. What do you think exposure to that guy will do to him? Either you say something to him or I will."

This was not the time to tell her about Barry's record.

"I know," he said, "but the man is lonely. And he's done a lot for us lately. He just likes to talk."

"Tell me one thing he's done that we didn't have to beg out of him. And what about Anne-Marie? He spends less time with her and their new baby than he does with us."

"What am I supposed to say?"

"I want you to draw the line. He gives me the creeps."

"I'll tell him to phone before coming over. Would that help?"

"Would that help?" she mimicked. "Don't use that tone with me, Peter, I'm not Sean. Just stop being so nice to him and maybe he'll get the hint."

* * *

Peter sat at the kitchen table giving Sean his bottle while Barry planed a door for their bedroom. It seemed that Barry and family were off to California in a few weeks, anyway.

"Ya, we pack up house and home, take the camper and work out there from October to April. Carpentry, fruit picking, that sort of thing. You folks won't have to put up with me this winter."

* * *

"What if something goes wrong here?" Colette asked when Peter told her about Barry's upcoming trip.

"He has someone who acts as a property manager." He watched for a hint of softening in her.

"Oh well," she relented, "it'll be worth it to be rid of him for seven months. Not long enough."

* * *

The day he returned from paradise, Barry said to Peter, "I'll get you a load of topsoil for that garden of yours."

"No, that's all right, Barry. You don't have to do that."

"How do you expect to grow anything worth a damn back there? That's just sand. I'll get you a truck-load tomorrow. Got a neighbour on the island runs a mushroom farm. Best compost you can get."

"It's okay, we don't really need it, Barry. The garden is doing fine."

"What, you and your little wife too good for charity?"

"That's not what I was going to say. You've done so much for us already. We'd like to try this on our own."

Peter picked up the watering can and walked back up the drive to the front door. Barry stood, smoking, staring down at the garden plot, taking the occasional long, audible draw on his cigarette until Colette returned home from school at dusk. When he left he slammed the door of his truck and squealed his tires into the lengthening darkness.

Three days later they found a pile of beautiful, moist earth at the end of the driveway next to the garden. Fat worms turned through the surface. Colette exclaimed and clucked happily. Peter hung back, uncertain whether he should reveal the source of the gift or let her think that he had arranged it.

Without warning, Barry brought them a squeaky tricycle for Sean, a gigantic piece of driftwood that he proposed they use as a centrepiece, clothes Anne-Marie could no longer wear while she was pregnant (which Colette immediately threw out), and great quantities of food from Wolfe Island. Colette was exasperated. She didn't think it as her place to stand up to Barry if Peter was not going to as well. She just wanted things fixed. Now.

During a fight over a faulty heating duct, they put their

names on a waiting list for one of the university-owned apartments west of the main campus. When one became available in early summer, they jumped at it.

"So, you're going," said Barry as he watched them load the van.

"Yes."

"Tell you what. Stay, and I'll take ten dollars off a month."

"We've already signed a lease."

"So break it."

"You could rent this place tomorrow. I know all sorts of people looking."

"But Buddy, they're not you. I like you and Colette. I can talk to you."

"I'm sorry, Barry."

"Fifteen."

"Why? You can tack that much onto a new tenant's rent. Get somebody in here quick enough and you've got yourself double rent for a couple of weeks."

"I don't care about that. I want you guys to stay. Somebody else moves in here and I have to figure them out. I've already got you figured out."

"We don't want to be figured out. We just want to be in a..."

"A what?"

"Well, a cleaner place, for one thing. And a safer neighbourhood."

"I see."

Barry lowered his chin and turned away. Colette watched from the front door. Barry glared at her as he continued, his eyes clouding.

"You can't do this," he said quietly.

"What do you mean we can't do this?"

"I thought you were my friends."

"Of course we're still your friends, Barry. Come and see us in our new apartment. We'll have a housewarming once we've moved in."

"I don't think so."

"Sure. Next week. We'll call you."

"No. You walk out on me now and you pay."

"Wait a minute," Peter said, but Barry was already in his truck and driving off.

* * *

That afternoon Barry telephoned the new apartment.

"Hello?" said Peter.

"Uh, ya. You coming back to clean up your mess here?"

"Barry? We cleaned before we left. What are you talking about?"

"I'm talking filth, man. I'm talking scummy carpets, grimy walls."

"Now wait just a minute. We left that apartment cleaner than it was when we moved in."

"Bull shit. You college types are all the same. You come in here and you live cheap and then you leave your dirt behind when you go. You're no better than anybody. Where would you be without me, eh? Where would you be without the roof I put over your head? You couldn't wait to get out of my dump, could you?"

"What do you want, Barry?"

"It took Anne-Marie and me four hours to get the place decent for the next tenants. Fifty bucks."

"Why did you bother to ask if we were coming back to clean, then?"

"Fifty dollars."

"Forget it."

"You think you're pretty shit hot, don't you buddy-boy? You think you can just crap all over old Barry. Well how about I come on over and give you and your sweet family a piece of my mind? You like that, Mr. Tough Guy?"

Peter hung up the phone.

"Who was that?" Colette asked.

"Nobody. A crank call, some weirdo."

Peter walked to the wall of windows overlooking the playground quad. A bearded man wearing a red turban was helping a little girl into a swing. The mellowing afternoon light signalled summer's close. The phone call receded.

Colette began washing kitchen cupboards and putting down shelf paper. She peeked out from the kitchen alcove. Peter was down on all fours and was looking into the cardboard mattress box.

"Are you stuck in there?" he said.

"No," said Sean.

"Do you want to come out?"

"No."

"What about supper? Take-out?" Peter suggested.

"Spaghetti and meat bulbs!" said Sean from his tunnel.

"Chinese!" said Colette.

"Right. Spaghetti and meat bulbs Cantonese."

It was a relief to get away. He jogged down the three flights of stairs to the front lobby and out across the parking lot to their car. Habit drew him back to their old neighbourhood. He found parking on Alfred Street and walked across Princess to the House of Peking. He stopped at the restaurant's entrance. Barry's black pickup was parked directly in front. How had he missed it? He turned quickly and walked back to the car without waiting for the light to change.

"I thought you were going for Chinese," said Colette when he handed her the bag.

"Lino's was having a special."

"Is everything all right?" she asked, dishing the spaghetti onto paper plates. "You don't look so hot."

"I'm fine. Just tired from the move."

"You should rest. You really do look wiped."

She had managed to assemble the bed while he was out, and the bare mattress was cool against his face.

* * *

"That was Barry on the phone yesterday, wasn't it?" said Colette in the morning.

"Yes," he said.

"What did he want?"

"He phoned to see how we were settling in."

"Don't lie to me, Peter."

"He had some questions about the way we left the place."

"And?"

"And we cleared it up over the phone. It's settled. Don't worry about it."

"Don't worry about what?"

"Nothing. I told him I'd go back and do some cleaning."

"And you're just going to give in? I thought we were through with him. Look, I have to get going. Promise me you won't do anything before I get back."

"Promise."

He kissed her goodbye and then went to distract his son.

"Side, Daddy? Side? Now?" asked Sean after Colette was safely out.

"Yes, get your sandals. We'll go outside to play."

"Kay!" he exploded. "Walk! Shoes! Side!" Sean ran madly down the hall to his new room. Peter rummaged in the hall closet for the child seat Sean used on longer walks.

They made the rounds through the playground from swings to slide to spring-loaded pony. Sean and Ibrahim, a boy his age from Ethiopia, tumbled down the pyramid together. Peter rubbed both their heads until Ibrahim's mother arrived and the adults talked awhile about how dangerous the play area was.

"I like the atmosphere here," he said. "So cosmopolitan. A good place for a kids, I think."

"Oh yes," the woman agreed, "but I'm a little concerned about the public schools here."

"I've heard good things about the local one."

"I would prefer it if Ibrahim wasn't exposed to...the lower classes," she said.

"But I don't think we really have classes in Canada," said Peter.

Ibrahim's mother raised an eyebrow. After a long silence she excused herself to rescue Ibrahim from the arch of a dome. Sean was pulling a little girl's hair. Peter moved him to the far corner of the quad.

"Time for a walk."

With Sean on his back, Peter walked down Sir John A. Macdonald to King Street and along Ontario. At the market, they were caught in a crush of end-of-season tourists. A shopkeeper gave Sean a helium-filled balloon, but the string slipped from around the child's wrist.

"Boon! Boon!"

Peter looked over his shoulder, then skyward at the spot of red growing smaller.

"Gone. We'll get you another one."

The Wolfe Island ferry pulled in just as they came to the dock entrance, trapping them at the stop light while an unbroken flow of cars disembarked and made the left turn into the downtown core.

He thought about heading home. Colette would be getting back soon and he hadn't done any unpacking.

"Let's get back. Mommy's probably worried."

Because he had the only key – the university had promised to provide a duplicate in a day or two – he had left the door unlocked but no note for Colette.

He turned and began walking back the way they had come. A girl selling flowers from a corner stand sold him an assortment of zinnias and marigolds. Tired, he got on a bus to shorten the trip. He sat Sean beside him on the seat.

The bus hesitated, blocked against the curb by a stream of traffic. He glanced around impatiently, reading the ads above the hand rail. Finally the bus began to move.

His eye was drawn out the back window to a red balloon bobbing up and down in the windshield of the vehicle following the bus. It was Barry, holding the string and smiling at him. Peter watched the truck until it turned down another street. The bus jostled from stop to stop. Sean slept slumped over in his pack.

At their stop, the bus lurched into the curb. He stood too soon and stumbled, grabbing the nearest pole for balance. Sean was awake but groggy. Peter stepped down, pushing through the double side doors. The instant they were steady again, he began to scan the parking lot. The child began to chant a shaky "ahhhhhh" as Peter raced across the lot. Their car was still parked in its space. Had Colette driven it to school?

He sweated under the exertion, laughing nervously as he shuffled, and Sean mimicked him. Once inside they would be fine, he told himself. There was still so much unpacking to do. The boxes would be a welcome diversion. His stomach hurt. He had to get Sean upstairs and fed. He would hug Colette when she returned, perhaps lure her into the bedroom while the child napped.

He was puffing by the time he reached the front doors. In the foyer, as he passed the wall of mail windows, he slowed to see if they had anything new. Nothing. An exit door opposite the main entrance looked onto a back parking lot, and as he passed he saw the black truck.

He imagined Barry inside their apartment, waiting for him when he got there, perhaps reclining on their sofa. Barry knew their furnishings. He would comment on the more spacious room. He would admire the parquet flooring. He would certainly be smoking.

Peter cursed again for not locking the door. He had not planned to be out for so long. It was supposed to have been twenty minutes.

Forestalling the inevitable, he decided to change Sean, crying and wet, in the washroom attached to the laundry room on the ground floor. The place was deserted. He took longer than usual to clean. The space was small and, except for the floor, it lacked a flat surface. As he knelt on the cool, damp tile, he willed the blood to return to his head.

Sean bounced to his feet and squeezed through the open washroom door to the laundry room. Peter watched him pirouette around the idle machines, happy to be clean and absorbed in his own magic. Sean found the garbage can and began arranging grey mats of dryer lint around the room. Peter spread himself flat on a bench and closed his eyes. He opened them when a woman entered bearing an overflowing basket. She didn't seem bothered by his presence or by the silence of the machines. He closed his eyes again.

"Just a couple of minutes more," he said.

When he awoke, a dryer was running, but there was no one else in the room. A blanket lay on the floor beside him. He bolted. In the lobby he stopped and called for Sean. People were drifting in from the day, looking at him, mildly attentive.

"Have you seen a little boy? Black hair, brown eyes?"

He took the stairs three at a time, slipping once near the first landing and banging his shin. The door to the apartment was locked. But how? Had Colette picked up the second key? He called but got no answer. Where was his key? Frantic, he rummaged through his pockets, but found nothing but loose change. Then he remembered he had slipped the key into the side pocket of the carrier, still downstairs. He cursed again. It was not until he reached the bottom that he realized he was crying.

Two girls with books under their arms asked if he was all right. He didn't know, he said. They watched him race up the stairwell once more, clutching the key. When he tried it, the key wouldn't fit. The phone was ringing inside the apartment. He steadied his right hand, willing the lock to turn. The momentum of the day, of the entire move, pushed him through the door. He could taste breakfast rising.

The phone stopped ringing. The boxes in the living room had been cleared and only a few remained stacked in one corner. It was four o'clock. He smelled ham baking, and potatoes. On the table beside Colette's cheque book was a picture drawn on a piece of graph paper, stick figures, a big person set to catch a smaller one coming down a slide. In Colette's handwriting was the message, "Look down, Daddy." He crossed to the window and looked down to where he could see Colette seated on a bench with another woman. Sean and an older child, the woman's daughter probably, chased each other up and down the pyramid. Peter waved to get their attention, but they didn't see him.

Something in the way Colette was sitting made Peter stare at her. The other woman was leaning in close, talking to her in whispers. Colette had her arms clasped tightly across her breasts. She looked cold. Only the occasional nod of her head while she held straight ahead told him that she was listening.

A noise made him turn back to the room.

Along the floor scudded a deflated red balloon. A full one floated to the ceiling.

He opened Colette's cheque book to the most recent page. The latest entry was dated for that day:

Ch#26 - Aug.6 - B. Carp - for misc. cleaning - $50.00

From where he was standing, he could see his reflection in the hall mirror. He stared at his image, the face puffy, the hair dishevelled, one shoulder sloped lower than the other. From the apartment below came the sound of voices arguing. He sat on the edge of the rickety coffee table, Sean's teeth marks in one corner, and put his head between his knees. He had nothing to give. He had forgotten the flowers on the bus.

perennial

At eight on Saturday morning Max Nazreen picked up Colin in the rental truck, and they drove to Max's brokerage to get his personal effects. Max's hair, now sprouting soft wispy black patches, had fallen out in a sympathetic reaction to his wife's chemotherapy.

As he unlocked the office door, Max said, "Chandra asked me to ask Beth not to come today."

"She did? Nothing could keep her away, Max. You know that."

"Oh, I know, and I told her that. She was adamant, though. She said she was afraid that if she saw Beth again she might not be able to let go, something about it being messy, wanting to drag a piece of this world away with her. Funny."

Colin didn't see anything funny about it.

Max grew quiet and his breathing laboured as they carried cartons down the corridor from the office to the elevator. The upper level of the mall was beginning to fill with shoppers.

When they arrived at the Nazreens', Colin got out of the truck and began to direct Max down the steep drive. The slope and design of the laneway demanded three tight turns, a difficult enough maneuver in a car, and Colin had to keep stopping

Max, sending him back up to make new approaches. He could see Max's bewildered face, as if just awakened by Colin's tentative voice.

Max had hired a man with a back-hoe to line the entire driveway with large boulders, and these now impeded the truck's progress.

"What possessed you to make the approach to your house so difficult?" said Colin.

Max climbed down from the cab, leaving the driver's door wide open and the engine running. He brushed by Colin, stomped down the pavement, and slammed his way into the house. Tim, married to Angela, one of Max's clerks, brought the truck the rest of the way.

Beth was sitting with Chandra on her bed, helping her sort through various piles of papers.

"What did you say to Max?" Beth asked him.

"I criticized his landscaping." He rubbed his hands as he looked around the room. "Put me to work."

"The best thing you can do for the moment is mind the children."

Max's brother-in-law, Gary, who had flown from Colorado to drive the truck once it was loaded, was trying to keep the children occupied in the living room. A large blue cartoon genie was singing and changing shape every few seconds despite an inattentive audience. Tim and Angela's youngest, Manny, began to cry inconsolably when Gary held him back from going into the kitchen to see his mother. Manny's wails triggered a similar response in Lori and Bim Nazreen, who darted past Colin in an end-run around the couch. Angela, wrapping china plates in newsprint, and Beth, sifting bills, wills, and homemade Mother's Day cards, came into the living room.

"We left you guys such a simple job to do," said Beth, shaking her head.

Gary left to help Tim load boxes into the truck. Colin ducked down the stairs to the basement. He picked up a box of seed packets and empty plastic medicine bottles on the way down. Max was hunched over a red tool box open on the floor.

"What do you want done with these, Max? I thought someone might trip on them."

"I know exactly where those are going," he said, taking the box and placing it beside the tools.

"Tell me where to begin, then."

"Everything stacked against that wall can be loaded onto the truck. Anything else is garbage."

Armed with this distinction, Colin began carrying the larger items – a floor lamp, a set of four kitchen chairs, a child's bicycle – upstairs. The children were colouring on large sheets of newsprint on the kitchen floor. Angela and Beth put cookware into boxes and dry goods into plastic grocery bags.

"There's an empty chest of drawers in Chandra's room ready to be taken outside," said Beth said as he passed.

Chandra was asleep on her back on the wide bed, the stacks of envelopes and manila files arranged on either side. She was able to concentrate only for short stretches now before having to rest. The papers around her were barely disturbed by the rise and fall of her breathing. Colin sat gingerly on the foot of the bed, and watched her sleep. Her deep olive skin, once glowing, beneath black eyes and an arrogant nose, was now like parchment. Her mane of thick black hair, tossed often in teasing dismissal, was now a cropped white cloud. The pupils of her eyes seemed almost visible through her onion-skin lids.

He heard Beth say, "Colin, Tim says he has room for that dresser now. Do you want help with it?"

He stood abruptly and the room grew dim. When she saw his white face she got him to bend down on one knee and lower his head.

"You've been going at it too hard, mister. Why don't you loosen that?" She unbuttoned his collar. "I bet it's pressing on your carotid sinus."

After a few minutes he regained his balance, and Beth helped him move the dresser out to the truck.

The rest of the day passed as if he were watching its grainy film projected onto the bare walls of the house. The new tenants arrived in the midst of the upheaval to swim in the nearby lake, and changed into their suits in the bathroom. When they announced that they had forgotten their towels, Max dug through packed boxes to find some. Another woman arrived to look at the kitchen table and chairs Max was selling.

"I really like the set," she said, "but I have no way to get it home. Can you deliver it?"

"No, I'm sorry, I can't," said Max.

"Most places deliver."

"I am not most places."

"Well, I just thought when I saw that big truck parked outside...."

"Madam, you go outside and look in the back of that truck. Look at how much bloody room there is in there. If I had room enough for a table and four chairs, I would be sending them on to Mile High City, now wouldn't I?"

The woman left without a word or a purchase.

Chandra called Max into the bedroom.

"How could you be so rude to that woman? Really! You bewilder me sometimes. And look. Look at the way you tied the armoire closed. The cord will scratch the finish."

"I'll put something soft under the rope at the contact points," he said, gently fingering the cord.

"Have you made arrangements for lunch?"

"No," he said, "no one seems to be hungry yet."

"I can't believe it. You're being a tyrant. It's inexcusable to make these people work so hard and not feed them."

"We'll get something delivered. Are you hungry?"

"You know I'm never hungry at this time of day. Another thing. The flight you booked for me is all wrong. I can't fly in the morning. I'll never be able to sleep on the wretched airplane in the morning. Get me a night flight to Denver, Max."

"I'll change it right away. Anything else?"

"It's time for my Sludge," she said.

Max went to the refrigerator and filled a glass with a thick, brown liquid that resembled chocolate milk. The drink was a bitter concoction made from a brown powder in a small plastic bottle, the same type of container Colin had found with the seed packets in the box on the stairs. It was a combination of four wild roots and barks, all native to North America, dried and pulverized. To mix the solution, the powder first had to be boiled in water for a number of hours, strained through a clean cloth, boiled again, and then cooled. It was named after a Canadian nun who had adapted a native Indian recipe to cure breast cancer early in the century. Each bottle cost fifty dollars and lasted about a week. Until recently, the Sludge had been a point of contention between Beth and the Nazreens.

Colin had heard Beth say on the telephone, "If you keep ignoring my advice I can't be your doctor anymore." Chandra kept drinking the Sludge and Beth kept driving out to the lake every evening to see her.

Gary announced that the Nazreens' refrigerator would have to be moved into the basement, because the tenants were bringing their own. While the rest of them leaned, sweat-stained and drooping, against various counters and doorjambs in the kitchen, Gary seemed to be just waking up. Angela was down at the beach with the children. Beth closed the vertical blinds against the early evening sun. She stood with her arms crossed watching Gary work with a large screwdriver.

"There's a good part of your weight right there," he said, leaning the door against the sink. All the food had been placed in plastic bags with each family's name labelled. Beth and Colin's, the smaller, contained food the children would never have eaten: jars of chutney, curry mixes, cans of mushrooms, sardines, pungent cracker spreads. Colin wanted none of it.

The four men shuffled with the fridge to the top of the basement stairs. Gary and Tim took the heavier end. At the bottom of the stairs the doorway was not wide enough for two to pass through at once. Tim took the weight as Gary crawled under the refrigerator and through the door. During this transfer the pair grunted and swore and laughed through gritted teeth.

Tim said, "You'll have to let me take it the rest of the way, Max."

"No," grunted Max, "You're my guests. I have to – "

"Move out of the way!" yelled Gary.

"I'm trapped here until you move," said Tim. "Gary can't hold that whole back end much longer."

Max let Tim take the weight and stepped back up the stairs. Expecting another step, Colin stumbled and sidestepped quickly to regain his balance. As he did, he stepped onto the edge of the box of seeds and empty medicine bottles. The contents flipped out, the seeds rattled, the plastic bottles bounced with hollow pongs around his shoes. His arms gave out and his side of the appliance toppled to the left. As Tim tried to correct the imbalance, Gary spat more profanity, and the whole thing crashed to the floor.

"How did those get back there? I moved them out of the way," said Colin.

"I know exactly where they're going."

"No, you don't. You haven't a clue where those are going. Somebody could've been hurt. Wake up, Max. Just wake up."

Tim and Gary righted the appliance and pushed it into a corner of the basement. Beth came downstairs and helped Max pick up the scattering of seeds that had burst from their packets.

"They're to go all around the property. Around the boulders. Soften the rocks a bit. I've known for a long time now where I wanted them to go. I just haven't found the time to plant them."

They wandered around outside in the falling darkness, picking up toys and crayons and bits of paper, looking for more to do. The truck could hold no more. Chandra's rocking chair would not fit, so she gave it to Tim and Angela. Max told them all to feel free to take anything that had been destined for the trash, but time was dwindling and to stay too long would be to risk being locked inside something dark and airless. They said their goodbyes quickly, and then walked up the driveway, past the van, to the parked cars.

Colin got in, moved the driver's seat back, and reached across to unlock Beth's door. She opened the door but didn't get in.

"Wait for me, please. I won't be long." He assumed she wanted to say goodbye to Chandra again. He rolled his window down and listened to the sound of her receding footsteps. From the dark came amplified sounds: water lapping at a dock, a dog barking from across the lake, pine branches rubbing overhead. The screen door opened and slapped shut. He listened for the same sound that would signal her return.

Finally he got out of the car and walked down the driveway, feeling his way from one boulder to the next. The truck loomed around the final turn, grinning with dim eyes. No lights were on in the house, but from a point on the slope to the lake came an irregular flash, and he walked towards it.

Max's landscaping plans had included an extension of the line of boulders along both sides of a wide path that led from the front corner of the house diagonally down through a series of terraced sections to the beach. Max and Beth were moving up from one rock to the next. Beth held the shallow cardboard box and a flashlight which she kept trained on the ground where Max sliced open a mouth of soil with a shovel. Beth handed him one of the empty Sludge containers which he dropped into the hole and tamped down with the toe of his shoe. After she sprinkled in some seeds, he removed the blade of the shovel and stomped twice to close the gash.

Colin knew they were doing it all wrong. Those seeds were much too deep. Max's technique was better suited to the planting of seedling conifers than to perennials. It would take a miracle for any of those flowers to show themselves in the spring.

"Beth, I thought..."

"Yes?"

"Nothing. Just wondering what you were doing."

"Do you want to help?"

"I don't know." He saw everything that she was then, everything that he loved about her: her capacity for love, her discontentment, her will, her patience.

"I think I'll just watch," he said.

calvino

One warm day in March, Howard found one of the students from next door smoking a cigarette in the sun on his side door stoop.

Her name was Lucinda Smythe. She was in her honours year of arts at St. Mary's University, and worked at the Barrington Street Zeller's afternoons and Saturdays. This occasional employment was what most interested Howard about the pretty, somewhat plump brunette, this and the fact that she sunbathed and smoked, a pairing of dangerous acts that Howard himself had been known to commit in his youth.

What his neighbour appeared to know about "real" people, at least the types who frequented her store either to buy or shoplift, was what Howard felt he lacked in his classroom. Had he known her better, and had he taught English or Film Studies or Social Work, they might have been able to collaborate on something, a dark novella, or a grainy black and white documentary, a ground-breaking political tract. But Howard taught Introduction to Electronics on Tuesday and Thursday nights to retirees like himself, and to the unemployed, neither group having much call for the honest grit and creative spirit Howard thought he recognized in Lucinda Smythe.

Lucinda's cat, Calvino, dashed into Howard's house whenever the door was opened. The cat, a grey and white male tabby, stayed for lengths of time inversely proportional to the temperature, and Howard's two grandsons, having been deprived of a pet, made Calvino's stays so enjoyable as to secure his return. So when Rachel, their mother and Howard's daughter-in-law, left in the morning for work, Calvino took her place. They played with him before school, and then, contrary to Lucinda's wishes, Howard would feed him some milk or cheese and let the grateful interloper curl around his pantlegs.

* * *

A couple of weeks later a spring storm dumped twenty centimeters of wet snow on Halifax. Lucinda had to push hard to open the side door of her house. Calvino stepped out gingerly, shaking his paws with annoyance. Lucinda was still in her bathrobe at eleven-thirty in the morning.

"No classes this morning?" asked Howard, crossing his forearms and leaning on his snow shovel.

She said she had quit school.

She said, "It's not as if I was going to do anything with my B.A., unless we're referring to the one I sit on all day. I had no job in mind when I started, if that's what you're going to say, Howard. No career path."

She was not going to spend the rest of her life working in a department store, she assured him. She was going to write a children's picture book about Calvino and herself. Howard expressed immediate interest. He told her that he had once had a short story published in the newspaper, back when he was first married and when newspapers were known to carry fiction in their Saturday supplements. The biographical blurb at the end of his story had read, "Howard Percy, a recent electronics graduate, would gladly waive the fee for this story in favour of a job interview." A manager at Nova Scotia Power saw the story and offered Howard a job.

"As a writer?" she asked.

"No," said Howard, "overseeing the night shift at one of the plants. I was with them forty-one years."

"I can't imagine doing anything for forty-one years," she said.

She admitted that she did not draw, but was signed up for lessons with an artistic friend who was "thinking about starting up a studio." As for writing the story, she had not put words to paper "as of yet."

"Not really important at this point," said Howard. "I have a friend, an acquaintance really, a writer who helped a cousin of mine with her first book. He would be a good contact. He's published picture books." Lucinda had never heard of him.

"Oh Howard, I'm not doing this for the money or for the recognition. You should know that about me by now."

He wondered what he really did know about her. She was usually alone. Her best friends were still the ones she had in high school. She was pleasant, sexy in a comfortably feline way. She let her cat have the run of the neighbourhood and then complained that people were spoiling him.

"We're getting on each other's nerves," she would say, as if referring to a lover. "When I want to sleep, he wants to play, and when I have to go out to work, he hides where I can't find him."

She had spent three years at university, but was now content to occupy her time showing sallow-faced women where to find black stretch stirrup pants and neon-coloured sweat tops, at least until something better came along.

Calvino leapt onto the roof of Howard's car and stretched his legs out fully, front and back.

"I think it's great that you live with your daughter and grandsons," she said. "I've only got the one grandparent left and she's in a nursing home. It's sad."

"She's my daughter-in-law."

"Whatever. Calvino, get down from there. You're putting paw prints all over the place."

"You don't think that's odd, me living with my son's wife and her children?"

"Are you kidding? It's way cool. I would so like to do that, live in an arrangement like yours. I mean, you get to say, 'I chose this. This is what I wanted all along.'"

"Aren't you curious about where my son is? Or his mother?"

"I figured you'd tell me if you needed to," she said. "Or if not, not."

* * *

In May, Lucinda announced that she would be moving back home to Yarmouth to live with her parents. When the boys heard this, they began to campaign for a pet of their own.

"I won't be 'lergic, I promise," said Brad. "A puppy won't make me do anything."

Wait until five in the morning, thought Howard.

Calvino's imminent departure and the boys' daily entreaties gradually lowered Howard's resistance, and he relented.

Returning from the pet store, he had to edge the car past Lucinda and her landlord standing in the driveway. Howard and Rachel began carrying plastic bags full of groceries into the house, as the boys fawned over the puppy, a beagle. They were going to name it either Betsy or Ralph, Brad insisting on the latter despite Geoff's assertion, supported by physical evidence, that the dog was female. While the boys began to argue about the name, a darker argument grew loud beside them.

"I can't believe you're doing this," said Lucinda, who looked to Howard as if she would either crumple in defeat or strike the man with her fists. The landlord, a tall, stooped-shouldered man named Petersen, said something that included the word "forfeit" and Lucinda threw her hands in the air in a gesture of incredulity, whirling away from him and then coming back.

"I so need that deposit," she said. "No way can I get by without it. I'll pay for the spraying myself. You can keep the interest on the deposit, but I just have to have that money back."

Petersen shook his head and walked back to his car parked on the street. Lucinda swore loudly and kicked the wooden garbage bin beside Howard's garage.

Allegedly, Calvino had brought fleas into the house, necessitating evacuation and fumigation. Lucinda looked so dejected, dragging a rolled carpet down the driveway and around behind the house, that Howard decided to cheer her up.

He handed her a book, a copy of Van Gogh's collected letters to his brother.

"I was thinking about your project," he said.

"Which one?" She prodded the decaying burlap underside of the rug with the toe of her shoe.

"The children's book. Your adventures with Calvino."

"Howard," she said, wiping her cheek with the back of her hand, "I think you can understand why that stupid cat of mine is the last thing I would want to write a story about."

* * *

The day Lucinda moved out, the boys let Betsy-Ralph off her leash and she chased Calvino up a tall tree. He stayed there while Lucinda loaded the van and then, when no one noticed, he disappeared. Lucinda walked the length of the street on both sides and through people's back yards, forlornly calling his name. Howard walked with her, and between them they asked at every house in the neighbourhood.

"How could he disappear like that?"

"I've heard that cats are smarter than people think. They know when plans are afoot," said Howard.

"He's mad at me for moving away. He's got a whole network of safe-houses here. Everybody feeds him. Would you want to leave if you were him?

"Look," said Howard, "give me your phone number and when he shows up, I'll give you a call."

Tears welled in her eyes. "You would do that?"

He said he would teach Betsy-Ralph not to chase Calvino,

or at least keep them apart, and if Lucinda could not return right away, then he would take care of him until she did.

She smiled and hugged him.

"Maybe it's better if you do hold onto him for a few days," she said. "This is not going to be an easy re-entry. The fewer trouble-makers the better, right?"

She thanked him for everything.

He said, "My wife, Sophie, died a while back. Her heart. My son, Geoff Senior, is an engineer. He works in Bahrain. Rachel came to live with me ten years ago after their marriage ended. You see, I started having panic attacks after Sophie passed. I would wake up miles from home without knowing how I got there or where I was. The first time it happened, the only phone number I could remember was Geoff's, but by then he was overseas. Rachel answered and she talked me home. She moved in to keep an eye on me. Whenever it happened, whenever I phoned her, she'd say, 'O.K., Dad, look around you, what do you see? Does anything look familiar? Are there any signs?' You wouldn't believe some of the places I woke up in. The lobby of the Dartmouth police station. Pier 21. An abbatoir out past Bedford. The freight depot at the airport. Finally, after six or seven times, I stopped blacking out, and nobody could think of a good reason for her and the boys to leave."

"I figured it was something like that."

Lucinda climbed into the cab of the van and drove away. Howard watched the brake lights flash on when she reached the stop sign at the end of the street. As the truck turned out of sight, Calvino emerged from under Howard's porch and headed straight for the front door. Then it struck him. Lucinda hadn't left her address or telephone number.

sarasota

Chafe had never been able to put away Christmas with the determination required to keep one clear eye on the New Year while lights, tinsel and baubles returned to their boxes. A rustling curtain or an errant spruce needle could set him festive again, and so he retreated while Patricia got out her step ladder. Nana Mouskouri sang two versions of Ave Maria. Patricia had a good voice, though untrained, and she crooned along in accompaniment. Chafe emerged when it was time to haul the tree out to the curb.

* * *

After work on Christmas Eve they had driven to the U-Cut farm near Clayton. She chose the tree. He told her that she had an artist's eye for symmetry. They brought it home secured on the roof of the car with yards of yellow rope tied in intricate knots.

They drank brandy and eggnog while they decorated. Between them they managed to break all four of the antique glass baubles Chafe had inherited from his parents. Perturbed,

47

Patricia disappeared into the kitchen. Chafe squinted to blur the colours of the tree, and the room began to sway like an amusement park. She returned with a needle and thread and a bowl of cranberries and popcorn.

"This is glorious. This is Christmas," he said, pulling her down to him, spilling some of the bowl.

"No," she said, "this first."

* * *

In the morning they were both sick to their stomachs. Chafe roused around noon and stole to the basement where he had hidden Patricia's gifts. He took the wrapped presents and the white plastic bag full of stocking stuffers, and went back upstairs. She was sitting pale on the couch. Beside her on the floor was her underwear still rolled inside her pantyhose. The lights of the tree were on. He told her not to look as he filled her stocking. She assured him that turning her head or any other part of her body at that moment was impossible.

"I thought we agreed not to do Christmas stockings any-more."

Chafe ignored her, whistling blithely "Good King Wenceslas" as he slid bath oil and scented powder, lacy black underwear, a red and white wooden spinner designed to resem-ble a hypnotist's aid, a crossword book, socks, and the latest Vogue into the bulging boot of felt, which his mother had sown, stitching "Patricia" in flowing script across the top. Of course then she had to push herself off the couch and fret around the house to find stuffers for him: a handful of unshelled walnuts, a candy cane off a bough, a small wrapped package transferred from under the tree, an unopened bar of soap lifted from the bathroom medicine cabinet.

He pulled each impromptu thing out with delight, exclaim-ing over it, slowing the process to a crawl. He conjured a man-darin orange from the toe of his stocking and peeled, sectioned, and consumed it before her very eyes. The fruit, bought just the day before in the crammed, frantic grocery store, was now a wonder in his hands.

"How can you eat that?" she said.

"It's magic, I'm transformed, I love you," he said.

"We missed a whole side of the tree."

"It's the most beautiful tree ever."

"You're becoming tiresome."

"I can't help it."

"You're not an eight-year-old, Chafe, and I'm not your mother. Everything you do does not delight me."

Then she made her way carefully, queasily, to the laundry room toilet.

* * *

They were hungry by the time his parents arrived for Christmas dinner. As the light faded, the thin colours of the day seemed to coalesce around the table. Patricia had bought tablecloth fabric especially for this meal, a deep wine red with metallic thread tracing a leaf pattern throughout. Against this were gold-coloured napkins. It had taken her weeks to find the right marriage of color and texture. Two green candles in plain pewter holders stood in the middle of the table.

His mother gasped when she saw the table. "Chafe, you never told me she was so talented."

Chafe's father said, "Something smells mighty good," Patricia's cue to disappear and tend to the bird.

"I'll help," said Chafe's mother, rising to follow.

"Margaret, sit down and have a sherry," said his father. "Give the girl some breathing room."

"You try wrestling a turkey that size all alone, mister. Let me tell you. I know."

But as Chafe had already gone to help his wife, his mother settled into an armchair, accepting a Dubonnet as consolation. She scanned the tree beside her.

"I don't see the Victorian balls we gave them," she said.

"He can put whatever decorations he wants on his Christmas tree. He's a man now."

"I had so hoped we could get through this without incident," she said.

* * *

Chafe felt his father's monologue coming all through the meal. Patricia was offering seconds of candied yams and mashed potatoes while Chafe stood brandishing the bone-handled carving knife.

"Still plenty of dark meat. Dad?"

"Oh, no, I couldn't. I'm still feeling the effects of last week's poker. Did we eat! Hell of a night, Chafe. Your old man cashed out big."

"No kidding. More wine?" said Chafe as he poured.

"I think I know two things for certain: no matter how much I try to lose, I almost always win; and nothing I win ever satisfies me."

"Which begs my perpetual question, Noah. Why continue to play?" asked Margaret.

"Let me revise. No matter how much I win at poker, I am never satisfied. And I am never really happy unless I am losing."

"I can understand that," said Patricia.

"Oh, then please, explain it to me, dear. This is one dark corner of masculinity I have never fathomed."

"If you lose, no one resents you."

"Precisely. Clever girl. A very perceptive soul-mate you have here, my boy." Patricia blushed but leaned in closer. He had her under his spell. "It's exactly that. When you are down on your luck, you know that your friends are rooting for you, in their straight-faced manner. There's no feeling like it. Furthermore, losing implies a change of luck. Therein lies the real source of all joy, you see. The change, that point at which one turns the corner and watches the wheel swing up, the smile return, that is the sought-after moment. To win endlessly is to lose hope, to tarnish, to begin to feel the others' eyes on your back. But to let a bloke lose it all only to slowly gain it back, well, therein lies the power."

Chafe watched his father's face, richly lit by the candlelight. More of his life had now been spent living away from this man than with him. Having been too young to enlist, his father became an undying student of that just-missed war. His friends were all veterans accustomed to long stretches away from domesticity. When they came home from combat, many sought the frontiers, the sea or the northern wilderness.

"We lived most of the year in tent camps, where we ate, slept, fought, drank when we could, shot bears, all the while mapping a battle plan against the rock, sizing up its riches. Gold, silver, nickel, cadmium, uranium.

"When it rained we played bridge, crib, poker, all day and night, under kerosene lamps while the airtight stove blazed against the downpour. That's when we thought about home, about women, hot baths, home cooking, family. It either kept a man sane or got him shipped out."

Chafe pictured his father, a lean young man wearing loose-fitting wool trousers tucked into rubber boots, a heavy leather belt cinching layers of shirts with button-down pockets. In his fist, like an extension of his arm, the handle of an axe held at the blade head.

"Surely this was what it was to be a man, out in the air, the unbroken vista before me, spruce and tobacco like a cologne on my skin. All my life I've tried to recreate that feeling.

"I know you've never understood that about me, Margaret. But this young woman, this lovely woman, our son's wife – no, don't look at me that way – she, she can empathize."

"You'd do well to ignore him, Patricia."

"There was no room to be cynical, you see," he said, addressing Patricia but looking straight at Margaret. "What we were doing, whether it was looking for gold traces in the clear streams or cutting gridlines or running surveys, was vital. No one was going to take that away from us. Not from these men who had endured so much for their country.

"I recall one man, Jock Hovey, saying to me, `When you get back down there to civilization and your sweetheart, Noah, you think about what you've been fighting for up here. By opening up this frontier, mining all the riches of this great land, you've been holding the line against laziness and ungodliness. Look what's ahead of you. Of all times recorded, this will be the best time to be a man.'"

Chafe's father emptied his wine glass. His eyes were damp.

"Dad, do you remember we'd drive north sometimes on a Saturday and tramp around the abandoned mines?"

Noah laughed. "You couldn't take the heat."

Chafe would follow his father, flies biting and branches slashing across his faces, his throat parched.

"Nothing like up North, boy," his father would say. "Look at that, schist, magnetite, pyrrhotite." He would break apart a hunk of weathered rock with the blunt side of his axe, and Chafe would look up for a clue. It was as if his father could see the rivers of molten rock, the folding, the faulting, syncline and anticline, all held in its clean face.

On road trips he would halt the car and scale cuts of salmon-coloured granite, his rock hammer stuck in his belt, traffic flashing by as Chafe and his mother sat waiting for him.

"A man carves his signature into the landscape. A man sets a structure against chaos. A man wills, and by doing so changes the very nature of space. Any more of this plonk?" he said, twirling the stem of his wine glass.

"The only thing I remember about all that, Patricia, is Noah calling out the car window, in a voice loud enough to crack glass, 'Where do the men go?' which means," she added for Patricia's benefit, although Chafe could see that his wife understood perfectly, "where do the men go to drink in this woebegone town? Where is the smoke-filled longhouse, the boat house, the sweat lodge? Where can I go to get away from the wife?"

"You lacked women friends, Margaret, that's all."

"I lacked a husband."

* * *

As she lay in bed that night, Patricia told Chafe she was afraid that he was going to turn into his father, but also that he would not.

* * *

Chafe bought a bouquet of carnations, pastel interspersed with white, and on the advice of the florist kept them in water overnight in the coolest corner of the basement. When he went down to get them in the morning, the cement walls were draped in perfume. He wanted to keep the flowers himself for their redolence of spring. Instead, he replaced the plastic wrap they had come in, dried the ends of the stems on a paper towel, attached the card, and got into the car.

His parents' high-crowned dirt road had not been sanded after the night's ice storm. He kept the car in the middle and prayed he didn't meet an oncoming vehicle. An empty white Ford Tempo was nose down in the ditch in front of the Jenkins', their only neighbours for a kilometer in either direction. Chafe slowed to look and, seeing no one in the car, continued. The approach to the house was on the down slope and he had to be careful to avoid skidding past the entrance.

His mother answered the door. "Happy New Year," he said, offering the flowers. She brought the bouquet to her nose.

She was dressed in a black and white plaid sports jacket, over a white blouse clasped at the neck, trim black slacks and low-heeled shoes. A suitcase stood just inside the entrance.

"You're going somewhere?"

"Carnations are a very smart choice," she said. "They keep for ages. Let me just put them in water. Can I make you a cup of coffee?"

"I didn't really plan to stay." He followed her into the kitchen where he handed her the packet of preservative that came with the flowers.

"Your father is out on an errand. He shouldn't be too long, I should think, if you want to wait for him."

"Where are you off to?"

"Some people just don't know how to drive in this weather. He's driving a young woman home. Did you see her car on the way in? Why someone would drive a white car in winter is beyond me. The tow truck will scoot on past it, I'm sure. Let me make you a cup of instant, Chafe."

"I've got to be on my way."

"But it would...I think he would be so pleased to see you here when he got back."

"We had made plans for the day."

"You must thank Patricia for the flowers. They're lovely."

"Actually, I picked them out."

"But here is her name on the card, signed by you, quite obviously – I do that all the time myself, signing Noah's name to cards and such, it's so much easier than trying to track him down."

"Will you tell me what's going on?"

"You don't think I meant, 'Thank your wife for picking out the flowers,' do you? I am fully aware of the capabilities of young husbands nowadays."

"Who is Dad driving home?"

"She reminded me of one of those girls from Personnel. They call it Human Resources now, don't they? You know the type who comes around with the card for so-and-so who is having her baby or getting married or retiring. By the time it gets to you the card is always crammed full with signatures and now, with this pretty and pleasant and efficient person hanging over you, you have to come up with something new to say."

"Can't you work this out?"

"Oh, I always work it out. I've shaken this marriage back into place so many times, Chafe, I don't care to remember."

"What should I say to him?"

"Why don't you remind him of his little speech. 'I'm never really happy unless I'm losing.' Tell him to chew on that one for awhile."

"At least tell me where you're going."

"I'll be at the Strathmore. Don't worry, Chafe, I'm not leaving for good. After two nights even the best hotel room begins to smell."

As he helped his mother across the slippery driveway to her car, Chafe saw Mr. Jenkins spreading salt by his mailbox across the road. His eldest son, daughter-in-law and two grandsons lived with him and his wife. The son was soon going to take over the construction business entirely. Jenkins was an amateur bird cataloguer for the Audubon Society both here and in Florida where he and his wife of fifty-five years wintered near Sarasota.

Chafe said the name of the place aloud. "Sarasota." It felt effervescent in his mouth, carbonated, like "Sarsaparilla," but with more of a pop. He said it again as he waved goodbye to his mother backing the car tentatively down the driveway.

He flicked the wind chimes over the porch, and went inside to wait for his father to come home. He wanted to hear more about the North.

**from where
i live now**

Daryl is trying to calibrate my sideburns with the tips of his index fingers, he's talking at me in the mirror, when he shifts his weight onto one hip and snaps his head like a tango dancer.

"Say, isn't that your wife?" he asks.

He returns his attention to my burns. I wait for him to pause with the clippers before I turn to look. It's M.J. all right, coming out of The Spin Doctor with whatsisname.

Daryl brings his mouth close to my ears and neck, and blows with little puffs at the clippings. Then he unfastens the velcro at the back of my neck, and flips the cover off, making it snap.

"There. You're free!"

As I walk ahead of him to the cash register, he puts his hand against the small of my back, and I fumble with my wallet. It slips out of my hand, dropping so that it's hanging from its chain beside my leg.

"Allow me," he says, reaching for it before I can react. He straightens up as he hands it to me. He holds it between his thumb and index finger. He's doing this twitchy thing with his lips. Daryl gives a good cut, there's no waking up two days later looking like a porcupine, but I don't need this.

They're gone by the time I pay Daryl and get out of there. I check in the restaurant and then head downstairs to the machines. We got in the habit, M.J. and I, of doing our laundry at The Spin Doctor even when we had machines just down the hall in our building. It's a good deal with the big screen and the coffee. It's always open and the guy's right there with quarters when you need them. You can grab a plate of potato skins and a draft upstairs while you're going through your cycle.

But I'm thinking, 'Where's the boy while his mother's down here rinsing out her panties with her new man? She's left the kid gawking at the tube, I just know it.' It's a Saturday, the day-care is closed. That's what sticks. Nothing else. I could probably meet the dude in a bar and fall in love with him. You know what I mean by that. This isn't about him or anybody else.

There's this chap I recognize, Yin Hua, one of the foreign students from where I live now. He bums a smoke off me and I tell him what I would do with a business loan. I'd start my own counselling service for kids. I guess I go on about it. He keeps nodding and smiling. I could be talking about dinosaurs. I'm distracted, though, because a woman at the dryer table keeps throwing me black looks, sighing, and slamming her towels around as she folds them. Yin Hua goes to check his load and the next thing I know there's John wrapped around my legs, and M.J. coming down right behind him.

"We left Buzzy somewhere down here," she says.

"That's interesting. Were you helping Mommy with the chores, John?"

"Yep," he says. I could just steal him away.

I straighten up with him in my arms. "I didn't see you come out with Mommy and whatsisname."

"His name is Ray. The boy was fine. I let Sara next door know. She looked in on him. Don't give me that look."

"Six years old, M.J."

"There," she says, pointing. "There's Buzzy. Over on that counter, John." He squirms to be let down, catches sight of his toy, and runs to get it.

"You could have left him with me," I say.

"He was perfectly safe, I told you."

"I'm two buildings away."

"You were out, weren't you?" She reaches up to brush at my shoulder. "Daryl always leaves hairs."

"Just give me some lead time. Call first."

"I don't like it that you moved so close. You're not supposed to see him except when we agreed."

"I can live any place I want."

"Lower your voice. And put that thing out. People don't come here to have their clean clothes stinking of that."

I butt out the cigarette.

"I'm thinking of moving out," I tell her. "To a quieter place. I haven't had a full night's sleep in months. The blind guy moved out yesterday."

"Why'd you move into that dump the first place?"

"Don't start with me," I say. "I'm just letting you know."

"Well you let me know first, please, before you go meeting him after school. I'm asking for that much. He doesn't understand about all this."

I don't want to get into a debate. It's easier to talk about other things, so I tell her about the blind man, my neighbour, Mr. Adekunle.

One day this dude comes to pick him up, a tall, churchy black man in a blue suit. He pulls up in a brown Pinto and gets out. He opens the hatchback and then goes into the building. I see this from my living room window. It's where I watch for John coming home after school. A while later the bro comes back with a suitcase and a couple of small boxes. He makes three trips in and out of the building, and then comes out guiding Mr. Adekunle by the arm. The only thing Mr. A is holding is his carved table lamp, the shade intact, the cord wrapped neatly around the base. He hands the lamp to the tall man, puts his left hand on the roof of the car, and lowers himself into the passenger seat. Then the driver gives the lamp back to him to hold on his lap. It makes me think of all he must have left behind. The braille labels that the superintendent put on the washing machine for him are still there.

"You can bet he stopped payment on his cheques," I say. "I should do that, too."

"Don't do anything stupid," she tells me.

I used to hold the front door open for him. I'd say, "Hello" and "It's Nick in 41." He'd always say, "I know that it is you, Nick," and then smile. We had this running gag. He would ask me how my work was going, and I would say, "Oh, it's picking up." Me with my orange vest and my hard hat and my rake, doing glorified yard work for the City. He never got tired of that one. But seeing Mr. Adekunle packing it in, that stuck something sharp in my heart.

The creeps in 39 made it bad for him from the get-go. There are the two of them rooming together, I can't even remember their names. One of them is worse than the other. Clumping up the stairs at three in the morning. Yelling outside on the street in the middle of the night, waking people out of a sound sleep. The way our building and the one across the street from it are positioned, it creates a canyon effect. There are the two of them and their buddy from the basement, the three of them work the same shift at the tire plant. Four to midnight is my guess, stacking radials, they're that swift. I should talk.

For a while there I was reading aloud for him. Articles on economics that he needed to know for his work. He never said if he was a student or a professor or what. He had a purple couch, two different upholstered chairs, a beat-up folding card table, the lamp that sat on it – I noticed he always turned it on, even when he was alone. He must have had a bed, too. I kept meaning to ask him about that lamp. He told me that the shade was made from the skin of one of his ancestors. I couldn't tell if he was joking. The lamp was turned on, the night I guess he decided to leave for good.

That's two nights ago. I'm out front waiting for a cab to the Palace, there's a gang of us standing under the overhang at the front of the building, the rain is pelting down. I like most of the kids who shack up there while they're studying and cooking and screwing and drinking and trying to postpone the inevitable. If there's one thing I'd give them all if I could – they're just sweet kids, the way M.J. and I were sweet kids when we first met – I'd give them a pile of money. A million dollars easy to start their lives with, and say, "That's the bundle, kids. Be smart with it." Or maybe I'd just give them all secure jobs. Forty-year, golden handcuff jobs. If not that, then something to hope for, something that would get them out of bed in the morning.

We're all standing around, talking. The band at the Palace is the same one that was there on the weekend. We all agree that it's a solid group. The kids tease me that it's past my bedtime, that I should try to make my way back up to bed, take my teeth out to soak, drink a cup of warm milk. Little groups of three or four dash out into the rain every so often to claim a cab.

Out of nowhere, it seems, this Mercedes sedan rolls up and parallel parks. You can picture it: Prussian blue, more car than any one person needs, the dashboard display lighting the driver's face an eerie green. We all know who it is, even though he will look the other way if we pass him in the hall and say, "Hello, Mr. Sengupta." He insists – I get this straight from the super – that he only represents a consortium of investors. Picture a black leather interior, black leather coat with a sable collar, gold rimmed glasses. Picture him checking us out in the middle of a rainstorm on a Thursday night. He gets out, walks down the sidewalk away from us, and goes in the entrance at the other end of the building.

A while later, when he comes back, he finds himself hemmed in by a cab that is double-parked waiting for someone named Brenda to get herself downstairs so that the rest of her group can leave. Cabby is honking his horn, buddy is yelling for Brenda, calling her "woman" and "bitch" and worse, as if he has the right to call anyone that, let alone someone he's supposed to be in love with. The rest of us are milling about with silly grins on our faces. I'm thinking that I should either walk to the Palace or go to bed. I'm too old for this. I'm wondering what John is doing. Is he sleeping or has he conned M.J. into letting him watch a show? Did he have a good day at school? Did he take the direct route home or the long one he and I usually take, the one that gives us time to talk? Did he ride his bike around the parking lot with the kid from his building, the one who is always being sent home? Mr. Sengupta begins to gesture for the taxi to move ahead. He slaps his hand on the hood. They are all still waiting for the someone named Brenda.

Instead of pulling ahead, the cabby gets out, followed by his passengers. They push themselves up close to Mr. Gentleman Landlord on either side of him as he stands with his back against his car door. He asks them to let him get into his car and drive away. They know who he is. They begin to tell him to his face what they think of his slum. The cabby is in no hurry, he hasn't had this much fun in a long time. He wants Mr. Sengupta to dance a bit before they part company. Touch my paint-job, will you? I can hear snatches of it, talk of roaches and garbage in the hallways and bad air.

Next thing, we're all down there on the street, quickly getting soaked, ringing that elegant vehicle that we'd give our eyes to own. The old gent holds his own, though, hand him that much.

"Where would you be without buildings such as this one?" he asks. "Just where did you expect to find suitable accommodation in this part of the city for such a reasonable rent?"

"Reasonable!" someone shouts. "You lock us into a year's lease! We're only here for eight months! Five of us in a two bedroom is the only way we can afford your reasonable rent!"

"I have to protect my interest," he argues, "the interests of the investors. Have you people no idea of the expense involved in running such a building as this? Let me tell you, then. Let me tell you about taxes, mortgage payments, salaries, repairs, heating oil, electricity. Perhaps you would be so good as to take this burden off my hands?"

Someone says, "Fuckin Paki, we oughta..." and he jumps on this. He's cornered and he lashes back. We're all racist, he accuses. We hate him for his skin colour. We are nothing but a hateful, racist mob.

Someone else asks him what he is doing here. Is he spying on us?

"I do not have to answer that. I am free to come and go as I wish. This is a public thoroughfare."

By now Brenda has arrived and is telling her friends to just get back in the taxi and go. The taxi driver agrees. We're all going to have to use the hand dryers in the Palace washrooms to dry our hair. No harm's been done. I mean, do you see the rest of us scraping together the down payment to buy one of these buildings?

The rain has let up a bit. The cabby says, "All aboard! Let's let the man get his door open now," when suddenly the creeps are there, both of them, and buddy from Number 11. They just seem to energize out of nowhere. Thursday night, going on eleven o'clock, they must have traded shifts with someone. And as much as three people can rock a Benz this size, they start in on it. Mr. Sengupta demands they stop, but three others who are still there because they didn't get seats in the taxi, join the fun.

I figure I have a choice to make. It feels like grade four again, being out in the schoolyard and choosing sides. I've had a few beers, I'm jazzed for a night of rock and roll. This old shitface has had it coming a good long time. We're just playing with him. We have the car bouncing pretty good. No way could we flip it, everyone knows, but he's fit to burst a blood vessel.

I begin to feel tired and wonder what John would think if he saw me involved in this. Then I feel the hairs rise on the back of my neck. I look over my shoulder and see Mr. Adekunle standing at his window. He can hear everything that's going on. Anyone who didn't know him would think that he's looking out at us. I know he's doing this so that we'll see him. His light is on. He told me that he likes to feel its heat on his skin, that he feels part of the larger world bathed in light.

"All right," I say to them, "cut it, guys. Cut it out now. That's enough," and one of the creeps looks at me as if he rec-

ognizes me, probably from the time I told him to shut his door
and turn down his Metallica at two in the morning, I wasn't pay-
ing to live in a college dorm. He tells me roughly the same thing
he did then. Then he sees me glance at Mr. Adekunle.

"I got no dispute with you," I say, and I step back from the
street. The other lads do the same, including buddy from 11,
leaving just the two of them pushing rather ineffectually. The
taxi is long gone. In the relative calm Mr. Sengupta gets into his
car and tears away. The creeps' blue language chases after him.
Mr. Adekunle's curtains are closed.

Next thing, he stomps across the shrubbery to Mr.
Adekunle's window, he has to reach up above his head, and
smashes his fist through the glass. Blood is streaming down his
arm from the wrist, he's laughing, he's so pisspot drunk. This is
too much for me. I walk up to the guy, he's got fifty pounds on
me easy, and I plough into his gut. It's like hitting a foam pillow.
He grunts and doubles over to get his breath, clamps his hand
over his wrist, and holds it all in like that for a minute.

"You're dead," he slurs when he gets his breath back. "You
and the fucking coon." The next day Mr. Adekunle moves
away.

* * *

"And that's how you left it."

"That's how I left it."

"He's going to kill you."

"That's what the man said."

"Get away from there, Nick. It's crazy to still be living
there."

"He won't even remember saying it."

"There's no reason for you to live there."

"Sure there is." She knows there is.

"No," she says. "No there isn't. Listen to me. You just don't
get it. First chance, soon's I'm done with this program, I'm taking John and I'm gone."

"With Ray?"

"Yes with Ray. Of course with Ray. He's just waiting for me to be done. So you see? You were right. You should follow your friend's lead."

"Why didn't you say something before?"

She calls John away from the big screen. "I'll call you, I will. I promise. From wherever we end up."

I look around the place after they're gone. There's nobody left I recognize. I'm out of smokes. My stomach hurts. The back of my neck is starting to itch. I think, 'Just wait. Somebody you know will come in.' But nobody does.

I go upstairs and stand outside on the sidewalk. I can see Daryl in the salon helping an old lady out of the chair. He's there early in the morning until late at night, six days a week. It's his whole life. He loves doing the old ladies especially. He loves his work, the whole package: haircuts and styles, perms and tints and tans, ear piercing, body piercing. The mirrored midday sun has lit his entire work area. I wonder if anybody has ever threatened to kill him. I think about it for awhile, and then cross the street to ask him.

a dying art

On her last assignment the teacher wrote that Lisa was writing not English but "Chinglish." I asked her if the professor was Chinese. She said that he was not.

One of the passages students were asked to write about related to the signs of craftsmanship evident in the English countryside. Even under foliage or in decay, structures belie the care of their construction. One of the words in the passage was "hedgerow." In China, fences are constructed of bamboo. I showed her a magazine article about the dying art of hedgerow maintenance in England. She pulled the issue towards her and began to turn the pages, looking intently at the lush photographs and illustrations. This was something she would like to try in China. Bamboo poles traditionally marked the boundaries of the rice fields, but these rotted and had to be replaced each season. I told her that some of these hedgerows were a thousand years old. The phenomenon was quite peculiar to England, probably due to the temperate climate.

She asked if she could borrow the magazine. "This will help me to writing answer," she said.

I edited her first draft and then her second. It was easier for

Lisa to talk about what was happening in her own life than be formally tutored, and so we reached an understanding: she would talk about herself, and when she was finished I would appraise her work. This suited me, as I prefer to work alone.

* * *

"These two passages give details about Nature, but create different kinds of pictures. Passage A creates a sense of where the layer of limestone, exposed by the quarry where the writer is standing, came from. I found these details easy to understand and was able to imagine the Dinosaurs and the Carboniferous forests. Passage B was harder to understand. For example, the writer describes the English farm technique of building hedgerows. Why would a hedgerow be tangled? However, I found an issue of National Geographic that contained details and pictures of English hedgerows. After reading it, I returned to the passage and found it to be a marvellous picture of Nature in miniature, revealing evidence of human skill in the rural structures built there."

The passages used metaphor to achieve their purpose. According to Lisa, metaphor as such did not exist in Chinese.

"But your culture, I always thought, is full of beautiful imagery. It makes me think of the most precise poetry. Don't you compare one thing to another in the Chinese language?"

Yes, she said, one thing can be said to be like another, but to call one thing another, to say that a field of grass is a sea, that is not possible. "Grass move like sea, but grass not sea."

* * *

"In Passage A, the limestone quarry where the writer is standing was once at the bottom of the sea. The rock is the result of living things, plants and animals, that lived millions of years ago. Today, the plants that grow in the soil

above the limestone are part of the cycle of Nature. They will
die, become part of the soil, and in millions of years, become
part of the fossil themselves. The writer uses the image of the
sea to show this never-ending cycle. When I read the passage,
I can hear the song of the sea, and feel the hills and valleys
made from the old ocean so long ago."

Lisa's daughter, Kim, speaks English like a Canadian. She is younger than my daughter, Christine, and last year was her reading partner in school. Once a week they went to the school library together, where Kim chose one book. She became easily distracted, and would often stop Christine while she was reading aloud to tell her about her cat. I have been up to their apartment. There was no sign of a cat. This year Christine is at a different school. Whenever Kim sees her, she stops whatever she is doing to run over and hug Christine, grabbing her around the legs.

Kim's father did not live with them. Lisa said that if he ever came around again, if he ever touched Kim again, she would call the police. She changed the locks on the apartment door at her expense.

Kim would not fall asleep at night until very late. Lisa would have to lie in bed with her, waiting, before she could do her school work. One night Kim refused to go to sleep and cried so hard that her neighbours phoned the police. Every time Lisa got up off the child's bed, she began to cry again. Lisa had to study for a mid-term chemistry exam in the morning. She screamed at Kim to go to sleep. When the police saw that Kim had bruises on her cheek and neck, they placed her in a shelter for abused children. On the third day, Lisa convinced them that Kim had gotten the bruises because of a fall in the playground at school. When I asked her if her husband ever beat Kim when he came to visit, Lisa said, "No, Kim just fall."

I listened to her without interrupting because I wanted her to feel comfortable enough to speak English. Sometimes I would miss some of what she was saying. She did not want to continue at university. She loved the study of chemistry, but the questions were always written out in long sentences. She spent more time deciphering the questions than she did solving the problem. It was too difficult. To make matters worse, her husband wanted to move back in with her.

She told me she had a baby before Kim was born, but it died.

"Was that in Canada or China?" I asked.

"Canada," she said.

"Did you report it to the police?"

"Yes. They say accidental. Crib death." She began to cry. "I know. My husband not care of it. Not feed or changing diaper. Letting die."

"Where were you at the time?" I asked.

"Away China," she said, "visiting my family."

In her teens Lisa had a lover. They worked in a Japanese tool and die factory in Shanghai. Lisa's mother did not like her boyfriend. To keep them apart she arranged a marriage to another man, the man who would become Kim's father. Lisa's lover went away to America. She hadn't had contact with him in years.

"He still love with me. I know. That five years ago. I already have Kim before he leave."

Her husband paid her $300 a month in support. She made $400 a month working as a nurse's aide in a retirement home. Her rent was $500 a month.

"What I should do? Should I quitting university? When I come Canada I only have middle school grade."

I knew what she wanted me to say. It was too much for her. She would fail again. She said she got a call from someone who wanted her to do sewing working at $8 an hour. I said it seemed a good wage for that kind of work and she should take it. She told me I was a very smart man. I gave good advice. She was going to take the sewing job, save enough money so that she could take Kim back to China to visit.

* * *

"*Passage B begins with the general idea that everywhere one goes in the countryside, one sees proof that people worked to build things such as roads, hedges, ditches, and fences with great care and skill. That skill or technique takes much practice. Even though some of the structures are now looking old and run-down or tangled with plant growth, that evidence of technical skill is still there.*

This passage is more interesting to me and has more to offer because the writer introduces new terms and techniques. For example, "metalled" roads are paved with crushed stone. The maintenance of a hedgerow is a very old and difficult technique passed on from one generation to the next. The skill required to care for the fields and meadows, maintain ditches, and build things like the old "ruinous" field gate, is considerable. The grey moss's vitality shows that every small corner is cared for. In the ploughed furrows, the copses of trees growing, and the harvest stubble in long rows, I can feel that technical skill."

Lisa talked about moving to Vancouver with Kim. There were no opportunities for her here. She looked into a course at a computer school, but the tuition was $6000 a year. If she worked six months and then reapplied, Manpower would pay her $1000 a month to go to the computer school. I asked what kind of job she thought she would get after graduating. It didn't matter, she said. "Anything better than cleaning up after old people."

Lisa was not able to pay for my help with her assignments. The last time she came, she brought a present for Christine, a cheap little ceramic village. Christine was all Kim talked about. When Kim was unsure about how to spell a word, she called Christine. I was known only as "Christine's father." I asked Lisa what her real name was, her name in Chinese. It is Zhaohui Li. Kim's name is Weirong Yao. I asked her why she had changed their names. "They tell me to when we first come Canada." Who? Who told her to do that? She could not remember. Someone in authority. English-speaking people have such a difficult time with Chinese words, she said, that it was easier for everyone this way.

While they were still married, Lisa's husband had a lover, a woman from Hong Kong, whom he later left for a British woman. Lisa said that she came to see this second woman to confront her and found her husband there in bed with her. The woman put on a dressing gown and talked to her kindly. She could see the woman's breasts showing in the opening of the gown.

Lisa decided to take the sewing work and save enough money to go to Vancouver. There was an uncle there. She was adamant that no one was going to pay her way.

I saw Kim's father for the first time when the elementary school was staging its Christmas pageant. We sat in the gym on old metal folding chairs. Every few minutes somewhere in the room a chair collapsed. The rivets holding the seat to the frame would pop and someone, usually a heavy man, found himself sprawled in the floor. We began to look around, trying to see who would be next, all the while sitting forward gingerly in our own seats. The costumed children trooped in, the lights went down, and we forgot about the booby-trapped chairs. At regular intervals, as the various classes of children took their places on the stage, a different group of parents armed with video cameras would leave their seats and come forward. Across the center aisle and a few rows ahead of us, Kim's father sat rigidly in his seat, staring straight ahead throughout each number. Lisa was not there. When Kim's class began to file in, he stood and walked to the stage where he intercepted his daughter. He stopped everything, barking orders and gesturing officiously as he got her to pose for a still shot. Then he recorded her walking across the stage, taking her place, singing. It was clear from the way he handled the video camera that he knew what he was doing. When Kim's class had finished their routine, her father walked back down the center aisle and out of the gym.

Lisa left Kim here when she moved to Vancouver. Kim lives

with the McLean family now, in a house two streets away. I saw them walking to church last week, Mr. and Mrs. McLean, their two teenage sons, and Kim. She had a new blue dress on. The McLeans are famous gardeners. Their yard is a showplace, not a flower or trellis out of place. I caught a glimpse of Kim's face as I passed. She didn't recognize me, but she looked well-tended.

home free

It was Monday, before dawn, and the snow snaked down the sidewalk in front of McKeown's house. Across the street a light shone in the rectory of Trinity Redeemer Church. The young Reverend Matthews had come to the door at breakfast one bright, warm Sunday in September to invite them to his service. A hand shading his brow, he had peered in on them through the screened kitchen door, addressing them as they sat over their eggs. Anne, indignant in her plaid dressing gown, told him he was rude to disturb them like that in their home, and closed the inner door in his face.

McKeown turned from the kitchen window to his bread, bending to sniff the breath of the sourdough sponge. He felt the cold kitchen floor through his slippers. The coffee dripped. He fed the fish their dry flakes that spread like snow across the surface until the tiny waterfall of the filter dragged them under.

He tapped the side of the aquarium. Harriet flipped, darting away in response. Romeo only fluttered, dorsal fin flat. These were the original sinners. There had been José, Jacques, and one whose name he had forgotten.

"Jacques died," his daughter Jennie had chanted for days afterward.

"You should not have let her see you throw the fish into the garbage," said Anne. "Now she thinks all dead things are thrown in the garbage. Sometimes I wonder if you think about these things."

He closed the dining room door. With a wooden spoon he whipped down the bubbly mass, releasing pungent gas that tickled his nose. He added a cup and a bit of warm water, a tablespoon of salt, stirred again, then poured in three cups of whole wheat, and then unbleached white flour, half a cup at a time, forming skin and flesh. Then he kneaded, working in an additional two cups of flour until it was smooth and elastic and not sticky. He saw with his palms and fingers, pushing from the shoulders, moving down along biceps, forearms, wrists, fingers. Only the very tips pulled to fold over the muscle of dough, coaxing it back.

All was still. He put the dough in a greased bowl, covered it with a cloth, and set it above the stove to rise. Then a draft rustled the curtains and cooled the thermostat, which kicked the furnace into a wakeful cough that blew stale, oily air into his face by the grate. The sound rattled up the vent into the chambers above. They were up.

"Good morning," he said. "Sleep well?"

"Yes," said Anne. "Cosy in bed, though. Hard to get up. Furnace is on a bit high, don't you think?"

"Mom, Jennie's got my book and she won't let me have it."

"Don't fight you two. Coffee left?"

"I'll put more on. Take this."

"No, it's yours. Jennie, do you have to go?"

"No."

"Then why are you clutching yourself?"

"Daddy will take me."

"Daddy's putting the bacon on now."

"No, I want Daddy to help me!"

"Do you mind?"

While they ate, Jennie and Sarah chattered. The radio alternated blather and music. He eyed the morning paper sitting in the mail slot. Anne held her coffee cup in two hands and did not let it rest on the table. She began to tell him about her dream. The wall of sound thickened. It became difficult to follow her story. Outside, snow was muffling the earth.

"I'm not going in today," he announced.

"Well...good. I mean, you're not ill or anything."

"I'm fine. I just need the day. I'll phone something in for the sub. I'll catch up on those essays I've been lugging around."

"Good. Good. You deserve it."

At eight, he saw them out the door. He sat and stared out at winter while his bread rose. When he took a first sip from his full coffee cup, the liquid was shockingly cold. He punched down the risen dough, divided it into three equal parts, formed loaves and placed them together on a shallow cornmeal-covered pan where they rose another hour. Then he preheated the oven and waited.

He ran his hands along the top of the stove, feeling where the heat seeped out and where it was still cold. A full morning sun began to warm the kitchen. The oven light flicked off. He sprayed the growing loaves, which lay fleshy and pungent on the stove top, with a fine mist of water, then slashed each with three cuts of the sharp knife on the diagonal. The skin of the loaves opened, three mouths smiling in each one.

He put his bread to bake, set the timer, and turned on the light that would allow him to view the browning. As he drew up a chair to watch through the stained oven window, he heard feet on the porch. A shadowy shape beyond the curtain knocked.

"Hello Sir," said a young woman looking up at him. She had a broad face and pale blue eyes set wide apart, and wore a camouflage-patterned hunting cap with the flaps down over her ears. A snowsuited child sat on a sled on the frozen driveway at the foot of the stairs. "Don't remember me, do you?"

"Give me a minute."

"That's all right. Martha Bonner. English class. Let's see, it would have been about eight years ago. I left early to have a kid."

"Well," he said, still not remembering, "would you like to come in?"

"Oh, no, we were just passing by and I said, 'That's where Sir lives.' All this time and I never just dropped by to say 'hi' or nothing. So, 'hi.'"

"Are you sure you won't come in? Your little one looks cold."

"Suzie? She's not cold. Are you Suz? She's used to being hauled around town by her mom. Bet you never thought I'd be somebody's mother did you?"

"Oh, I don't know about that." He wished she would come inside or leave.

"Had a heck of a time getting over that pile at the end of your driveway. You need somebody to shovel it out for you?"

"No. As a matter of fact I was just going to get at that." He saw disappointment change her face. "What do you charge?"

"For a driveway this size? Fifteen."

"Fifteen dollars?"

"Aren't you working today or do you teachers have one of them P.D. days?"

"I'm...working at home today. There's a shovel in the shed. The door should be open."

"Thanks. I didn't bring mine. To tell you the truth, I wasn't sure you'd go for the idea, especially it being me and the way I used to act up in class and all. You mind watching Suz? She's a real good kid, won't give you a stitch of trouble."

"No, that's fine."

Suzie refused his gesture of help, removing her toque, boots and snowsuit jacket by herself. She stood pale and patient in sock feet and knee-worn snowpants. He heard Martha beginning to scrape outside.

"Would you like something to drink?" Suzie shook her head no. "Hungry? Can you smell that bread baking?" Her face softened. "It'll be ready in a few minutes." She climbed onto a kitchen chair.

"Say," he said teasingly, "shouldn't you be in school today?"

"Shouldn't you?" she replied.

He took a deep breath and closed his eyes. The buzzer on the stove sounded. Grateful for the interruption, he took up the oven mitts and bent to remove his bread to the wire cooling rack on a side table. Through the kitchen window he could see Martha marching back and forth like a rink rat across his driveway, the shovel canted expertly.

The smooth scraping changed to an irregular hack and chop as she swung the shovel against the frozen embankment left by the plow. He watched her throw the implement down after a moment and return to the kitchen door.

"That's solid ice. You got a smaller shovel or an axe or something?"

"No, I'm sorry. I usually get at it right after the plow goes by."

"Even at night? Three in the morning you're out there shovelling."

"No, of course not in the middle of the night."

"You were always doing that," she said, closing the door behind her as she came inside. The snow from her boots made a brown puddle.

"Doing what?"

"Oh, telling little lies in class. Not big ones that could land you in trouble or anything, but little stretchy ones. One thing's for sure, Suzie here's not gonna have to read that shit you made me read, excuse my French."

"Well that's just fine and dandy," he said, reaching for his wallet on the kitchen counter. "Fifteen dollars was it?" She took the bills.

"She's going to the new Christian school they're building up the next concession line. Know the one? They won't have no books that take the name of Our Lord in vain. No teachers playing around with the truth."

"That's just about enough, young lady."

"Hear that Suz? That's just the way he used to talk to me in class. Well I'm not one of your prisoners now, Sir."

"I don't remember teaching you. You were never in my class."

"See how he twists the truth? Just the way Reverend Matthews said. Just yesterday in bible study and after, when we were outside saying goodbye in the parking lot where we could see across to your house, he said to me when he spotted you in the window, he said, 'There's a man who could do to feel the word of God.' You should come listen to what he has to say. He's a very smart man and not that much older than me. Can you believe it? Somebody that young and so smart. You don't go to church do you Sir? You should come across next Sunday. Bring the family. Come and hear Reverend Matthews preach. He's sure to raise the spirit in you."

"All right, fine. I will. Next Sunday."

"Oh, I know you're only saying that to get rid of me, but you should consider it. Lord knows you're in dire need. I mean, look at you, playing hooky from school, hiding from your obligations. Sure, you should come across. We all bring something for Friendship Hour after the service. You could bring a loaf of your nice bread. Suzie, get into your coat and boots now, honey. Don't step in the wet there. That's a good girl. Well," she said as she stood again after crouching to help the girl into her coat, "it was good to see you again, Sir. I'm real sorry —embarrassed, I'm real embarrassed I've forgotten your name. Here I've been calling you what I used to call you in school.

"McKeown."

"That's right. Mr. McKeown. Well...thanks for the work, Sir."

* * *

For the next two hours he stared out the window. He didn't bag his bread, he couldn't bear to look at the essays he had brought home to mark. He listened to the noises of the house: the furnace flipping on and off, the beams cracking in the cold, the whir of the aquarium pump. The earth continued to fill with sepulchral snow. He felt like a robbery victim, but he couldn't say what had been taken from him.

He put on his coat and boots with the intention of walking around the block. The exercise and the cold air would clear his head. Perhaps he could salvage something of the day. But instead of turning down the sidewalk, he crossed the street and went into the church. Climbing the stairs to the rectory, he felt the day's aimlessness solidify. He wasn't sure what he was going to say. He was either going to give the minister a piece of his mind or give himself to Jesus.

It would depend on the look on the young man's face.

**someone you
can count on**

Jamie considered nothing, save a cornfield after harvest, to be lonelier than an empty school. He leaned forward, turned over a journal lying on the coffee table before him, and let it drop. He leaned his head back against the padded cushion of the couch, propped his shoeless feet on the table, and closed his eyes.

Two men entered the staff room. The first was Hank Green, a large, affable man in shirt, tie and an open spring overcoat. The second, Bruno Poirier, was thin, dark-haired, sharp-featured. He wore a mid-calf brown leather coat over jeans and sharp-toed cowboy boots. At his neck was a string tie held with a golden eagle clasp.

"My hands are tied, Bruno. They have to look at the P.P.1 list first for returnees coming off leave and others wishing to transfer, then P.P.2. And that list is about as long as...well, you know the procedure."

Hank switched on the light. If he was startled by Jamie Kerwood sitting there in the dark, he did not show it.

"Procedure?" said Bruno. "You're talking to Mister Procedure here."

Hank flipped through the papers in his mailbox, arranged them neatly on top of the books he was holding, and placed the stack on a work table. Bruno shoved his mail back into the box and slumped into the nearest armchair.

Jamie, his eyes still closed, said, "Who are you today, Bruno?"

Hank walked by holding two empty glass coffee pots in his hands and said, "It sure would be nice, just one morning before I retire, just once, to come in here to see the coffee made. You young guys..." He laughed to himself, shaking his head, before disappearing down the dark passageway that led to the main office.

"I'm Jack Henderson today," said Bruno. "What I would give not to have to face his bunch of hyenas."

"Could be worse. You could be in for me."

"You're here early. You usually come in this early? Me, I make sure I'm always the first smiling face the custodian sees in the morning. He's the one you have to impress, not the principal."

Hank returned with coffee pots filled and said, "Ha! Your smiling mug?"

"I saw the geese coming home this morning," said Jamie, sitting up. "I followed them in. For two, three full minutes they just hovered close over the car. I could feel them. Their wings beat like a bellows. And the noise. The way they gab to each other. It felt like I was flying along with them."

"I've never seen you in this early," said Bruno. He sniffed the air. "Something a little off in here?"

Hank turned to Jamie. "Where are you with the elevens these days?"

"'Tomorrow and tomorrow and tomorrow.'"

Bruno rose and walked back to the mail slots, peering inside without removing anything. "Jack has left me without a weapon again. It's crucifixion time. You guys will have to come and watch. Period five. Cripes, Jacko, just once I wish you'd prep a lesson or two."

"I'm still on the précis, myself," said Hank. "Hoping to start *Macbeth* by early next week. You need work sheets or anything like that? Just got this great package in from the States. Multiple choice tests, answer sheets, study questions, transparencies. Just about everything you'd need. Hmm?"

"We're almost done," said Jamie.

"How's that mother of java coming?" said Bruno, crossing to check the dripping fluid.

"Now watch it. Don't pull it out until it's finished dripping. The last time, you pulled it out while it was still dripping."

Bruno, ignoring Hank as he walked away, said, "I'm trying to remember what we studied in school. *Hier les Enfants Dansaient*, now I remember that one. And *Les Belles Sœurs*. I mean...plays! Politics! October 1970. We talked, we argued. It lived for us. You know? And none of this teacher-has-the-only-answer crap, either. If the prof didn't know what he was talking about, we damn well let him know. Not like here, I'll tell you. Not like here."

As Bruno was speaking, two more teachers came in, Kate Wilson, in her mid-twenties, dark-haired, bright-faced, still looking expectant and purposeful after two years of teaching, and Helen Gill, pushing fifty in a sober suit, a veneer of calm and a wry smile belying dread of the day ahead.

Helen, who liked to stir the pot, said, "Oh no, here he goes again. Wind him up."

"You folks are lucky I don't teach here full time," said Bruno. "There'd be shakin' in the halls and rockin' in the aisles, I tell you."

Kate said, "Has anybody seen the schedule for today? We're supposed to have an assembly in the morning but I haven't seen anything yet." She crossed the room to the coffee machine.

"Juniors at 9:40, seniors at 10:35. There's a supervision roster. You're guarding exit E, I believe," said Hank.

"Bruno, if you come on staff here, I'll tender my resignation immediately."

"I love you, too, Helen."

"The coffee's tepid!" said Kate. "I hate that. Who forgot to turn on the switch?"

By now four or five other teachers had come in. Jamie had not moved from his seat. He said, to no one in particular, "If I could fly I would be a condor majestically riding a current of mountain air."

"He's still on the geese," said Hank to Helen as he sat beside her.

"How's that?"

"Canada geese. They're beginning to come north again. He saw them driving in this morning. He should be preparing his lessons."

"I know what he's thinking about," said Bruno. "Nineteen, honey-blonde, gimlet-eyed, answers to Susie Rothesay. Am I right? What? Huh?"

"You're not involved in anything...unprofessional, now, are you, dear?" said Helen.

"Of course he's not!" said Hank.

"And I was so hoping for a juicy morsel to go with my coffee."

"Thirty minutes to hell, people," said Bruno. "Anybody want to make an easy ten bucks and take Jacko's lovelies for me today?"

"Listen," said Jamie.

"...cheque deposited every two weeks instead of monthly, you save seven years on a twenty-five year mortgage," Hank said to Helen.

Again Jamie said, "Listen."

"Listen to what? Nobody's listening," said Bruno.

A female voice over the public address system broke in. "Mr. Collins. Call on line one. Mr. Collins."

"Can't you hear it?" said Jamie.

"No, what is it? What do you hear?" said Kate. She paused and then moved off to the photocopier.

Bruno was saying to Helen, "We didn't dare talk back to a teacher the way that...that tête carré, whatsisface, the one with the sister – you know them, the twins..."

"Pearson."

"Whatever. That little pustule told me to you-know-what the other day when I was in for you, just under his breath, loud enough for me to hear. I tell you, if I was on staff here..."

Kate banged the side of the photocopy machine with her foot. "We're out of toner! Why does this always happen when I've got sixty copies of a test to run ten minutes before class?"

Helen turned to Jamie. "Don't you teach first period?"

"Behind it all," he said. "Can you hear it? A bellows. The world, breathing. It never stops."

"I've got to see Albert about a film projector," she said as she gathered her things and stood. "Are you all right? You've hardly opened your eyes the past twenty minutes." She waited, then walked away.

Hank said, "It hasn't been that long, Helen. You got here at 8:12 and it's now," as he checked his watch, "8:21."

Bruno filled his coffee mug. "One more for the road. Or should I say "last walk" down Executioner's Row? My offer stands. Anyone? Anyone?"

"I'll take it," said Jamie.

"You're not teaching period five?"

Hank said, "He's pulling your leg. I know for a fact that he's got keyboarding period five. He can't take your class. Besides, your occasional teacher's contract says – "

"Stow the contract a minute, all right, Hank? Now, tell me again, James. You teaching period five or what? I'd owe you. I'd owe you big."

"As I was driving I watched one goose at the tail end of the skein. It was tough keeping the car on the road and watching the birds at the same time. It was beautiful. I was flying with them. The last bird was so close to me that I could have reached up and touched him. I didn't seem to bother them. It wasn't as if they were preparing to land. They maintained the same height above me, right down the center of the road."

"This one's burnt," said Bruno. "He's not even listening. I

must see this kind of thing twice a week at least. Say a prayer for him. What am I doing in this racket, anyway? At least I don't have to mark," and he walked off to first class.

"You want me to cover your home room for you?" said Hank, worried.

"The last bird was continually playing catch-up. He was weaker than the rest of the flock. He would lag, falling back a few spaces, then work and work to pull himself back up in line. Then he would fall back again. This must have gone on for a full minute."

Hank stood, lifting his neat pile of papers and books. "The bell's going to ring. Are you sure you don't want somebody to take your home room? I think someone ought to tell Don." To Kate as she walked past, he said, "Is Don in yet?"

"I'm late, Hank," she said.

"'Catch up,' I kept calling to him. 'You can make it.' It was incredible. 'Catch up. Go, go, go, yes, you can do it.' An invisible thread kept drawing him in and then playing him out as if he were a fish on a line. I was hunched over the wheel, right up with my chest against it, straining to keep my eye on him, whispering encouragement. 'Catch up, catch up, catch up.' All their necks were straining, straining toward home. 'Catch up. Close ranks.'"

Hank said, "I've got to go," but remained standing, looking down at his shoes.

The sound of the first few bars of the national anthem broke over the P.A. system. Hank straightened. Jamie did not move. They remained motionless and awkward, Hank glaring at Jamie throughout, until the music stopped.

"You could at least've stood."

"While there's still a country to stand for, Hank?"

"You know, I think you are a good teacher, potentially a great teacher, but your attitude over the last few months..."

"Everybody in my homeroom talks through all of "O Canada". It used to bother me, but after a while I began to think, well, that they're talking to each other. The geese talk the whole time and they still get where they want to go. In fact, I bet they wouldn't all make it unless they honked to each other, sending messages up and down the skein. 'Turbulence ahead. Bank fifteen degrees here. Watch for hydro wires ahead, one hundred meters.' "

"You still have time to make it."

The school secretary came in and stopped beside the photocopier. She said, "Mr. Kerwood, one of your students just called down from your room. Is no one taking your home form this morning?"

"Attendance cards are in the top right hand drawer, Lorraine. They're a fun bunch. Not very patriotic, but fun."

She turned on her heel and walked back down the passageway to the office.

Hank said, "All right, here's what we'll do. We'll cancel your next two classes. Give you some time to pull yourself together. This kind of thing is more common than you'd think. One day you're sailing along at full throttle and the next your fuel line is clogged. You just need some down time, a couple of hours. Or maybe Bruno can take...What do you teach second period? I think Jack has a spare."

"This was all at dawn, mind you. First light. Like the feeling coming back in your arm after it's fallen asleep. I was driving before the sun was up. Wide awake. Four in the morning."

Lorraine came back with the school's principal, Don Gordon, an imposing man whose appearance suggested physical prowess and high standards.

She said, "He hasn't moved."

"Mr. Kerwood, may I see you in my office when you have a minute?"

Jamie nodded and murmured. Don poured himself a cup of coffee, pausing to evaluate the situation, then left, followed by Lorraine.

"So, I was cheering, 'Come on, do it.' Then I was looking at the ditch head on. 'Whoa, get her back on the road, there, James,' I said to myself. The tires were chewing gravel. Then all of a sudden it struck me, 'What are you doing? This is killing you. Take it down a notch. Gear down, old tail-end gunner. Pace yourself for awhile. I mean, how do you know you're even going in the right direction?' "

Don's voice came over the P.A. "Mr. Green still there?"

Hank said, "Yes, Mr. Gordon."

"Mr. Green, perhaps you could impress upon your colleague that he has a class of 29 grade ten English students waiting upstairs for his professional tutelage and that if he fails to carry out his contractual obligation within the next two minutes he will have breached said contract."

Hank said, "You heard him. Don't blow it."

Jamie reached behind the couch and picked up a pair of muddy hiking boots and began cleaning them with a pencil over the coffee table.

* * *

When he looked at the clock again, it was 9:20. He was lying across the length of the couch, his fingers interlaced over his eyes. He heard a knock at the door. He looked in its direction, but did not move. The door opened to Susan Rothesay, as Bruno had described her, wearing a winter coat.

"Hello, Susan."

"Hello," she said. "Is Miss Wilson here?"

"I don't think so."

"Either she is or she isn't."

He glanced over his shoulder. "Isn't."

She held up a notebook. "Can I put this in her mailbox?"

"Sure," he said, then, teasingly, "and where should you be right now?"

She came in and found the right mail slot. "I could ask you the same thing. Where were you? Mr. Gordon came and dismissed the class."

"Waylaid, I guess. Are you heading home?"

"Yours is my only morning class on Day Two. I could've

stayed in bed."

He said, "Want a coffee?"

"I don't drink coffee," she said warily.

"Come in and talk to me, then. Don't stand in the door-way."

"O.K., but I can only stay a few minutes." She sat in the nearest chair. "That's Mr. Green's line."

"What's that?"

Imitating an overly dramatised plea, her arms flung wide, she crooned, "Tawk tu meee!"

He laughed. "Perfect!"

"One guy answered a question correctly from outside the window last week without Mr. Green even knowing. He just kept writing on the board."

Lorraine came in to use the photocopier. When she saw Susan she threw her a disapproving look.

"Are you sure it's all right for me to be in here?"

"I wouldn't worry about it."

The bell rang. Hank came in, followed by Bruno.

Hank said, "You still here? Have you talked to Don yet?"

Jamie ignored him. "You know, Susan, I never expected to be someone people would come to depend on. I thought that if I just kept on going the way I was going, I would fade away so gradually that no one would ever notice."

Bruno said, "Is she allowed in here? I didn't think students were allowed in here."

"I think you better skeedaddle, young lady," said Hank.

Jamie said, "You just stay where you are, Susan." Firmly, to them, he added, "This happens to be a teacher-student confer-ence."

"I think it's only fair to tell you that Don wants you off the property," said Hank.

"Nice of him to say so himself. Susan, keep your eyes wide open. You'll see that nothing just fades away. Anything that passes always brings something of the world down with it."

Bruno traced a circle with his finger in the air beside his temple.

"When I was in grade nine, my locker was beside Angelica Fellucci's. She was in grade twelve...a woman. I was in love before I'd even talked to her. I became obsessed with the idea of giving her something, a special gift, one that would suit her. My gift had to be something matching her thick black hair, her spicy breath, her voluptuousness. I went directly from school one day to an imported food shop where I bought her a brick of Gorgonzola cheese. Having never tasted it, I was basing my purchase solely on the name. Gorgonzola. Angelica. She would see immediately how sensitive I was. When I arrived at school the next day, a Friday, she was there combing her lustrous hair in the mirror on the inside of her locker door. She smiled, said hello as she always did, and I handed her the package. Not waiting for her response, I darted off to my first class. I didn't see her for the rest of the day, and after school walked home, daydreaming about her. When I got home, my mother was watching the television and crying."

"I think I'd better go now," said Susan.

"Please stay. I'm trying to make sense of it. In school we gave oral reports. Pollution – every second one was on pollution – if left unchecked would be the end of life as we knew it. More people die each year in auto crashes in North America than died in all of World War II. If you become a popular politician, someone with a gun will shoot you. Nowadays the native hue of resolution can usually be found in a bar somewhere, sicklied o'er with the pale cast of thought. If left unrefrigerated overnight, say in a school locker, Gorgonzola cheese outlives its welcome, even as a gift of love. I mean, tell me what I'm supposed to do with this. I didn't ask questions like this when I was eleven. I'm asking them now."

Susan stood and took hold of his arm. "Come on, Sir. Let's get out of here."

He remained seated. "The world turns its pockets inside out for answers. I watched a beautiful goose turn into a hill of dirt."

Hank exploded with indignation. "You're supposed to be

teaching, dammit! There's no backbone left in this place. You have a job to do. This young person needs you."

"She doesn't need me. She needs someone who can sort grades, keep people quiet and orderly. Right, Susan?"

"No. Not just that."

"Our students have heard enough from us. They know enough to turn their faces away from the mess."

Then Don Gordon walked in.

"Mr. Kerwood, as far as I am concerned, your contract with this board is terminated. Please leave the building."

"Don't worry, bub," said Bruno. "They can't really do this. The federation is too strong. Maybe a slap on the wrist and a brief suspension at the most. Believe me. He's just trying to scare you."

"You keep talking like that, Monsieur Poirier and this will be your last call as a substitute to this school."

Kate came in and immediately checked her mail box. "Doesn't anyone teach in this school anymore?"

Don said, "We're waiting, Jamie."

Bruno whispered, "Don't let him intimidate you."

"Do what he says, Jamie," Hank urged him. "Don't make it any harder on yourself than it is."

"Will somebody please tell me what's happening?" said Kate.

Then Jamie bent, reached under the coffee table, and pulled out a full, green plastic garbage bag. It sagged as he lifted it. The look on his face suggested that it would explain everything.

Susan said, "Out of all you, he's the only one who should be here."

Don said, "Get her out of here."

Hank made a move to take her arm, but she danced out of reach. They watched as she side-stepped between the coffee tables and slid into the unoccupied space beside Jamie. She locked an arm around his and smiled defiantly.

"Young lady, you have just earned yourself a suspension," said Don.

She ignored him. Jamie turned his head to look at her and let the weight of the bag settle on the table.

"He must have heard me talking to him, because the next thing he did was bank off from the formation. I slowed the car, watching as he came down in a bare field. I pulled onto the shoulder and got out, stumbling down a steep incline and up the other side of the ditch. I straddled the fence, careful on the rusty barbed wire. He was standing in the open in the middle of the stubble of old corn stalks. He could see me walking towards him, but stood perfectly still, watching me, waiting. He was not frightened but quiet and dignified. He scared me, hissing. I slowed my pace, trying to be quiet, quiet, picking each step carefully around the clods of mud and the corn stalks."

Hank said, "What's in the bag, Jamie?"

"The bird stopped hissing and put his head down on his chest the way a swan will. He sat, folding into a hummock of dark feathers. Trying to sink into the dirt. I was twenty meters away. I called to him, 'Get up,' I told him. 'I didn't mean for you to stop altogether. You have places to go. Get up. Fly. You're almost there.' But he was not moving anymore. Then I noticed shadows from behind me, long, faint shapes in the dawn. Crows, sashaying over from across the road. I turned to look and there they were: three laughing undertaker crows. 'I didn't mean just drop out of the sky and die. Get back up there. All I meant was take it easier. Catch your breath.' "

For seconds all was still. Then Lorraine said over the P.A., "Please excuse this interruption. Would all members of the junior girls' volleyball team please go to room 103 immediately to have their pictures taken. That's all members of the junior girls' volleyball team."

Bruno whispered to Hank, "This guy is cooked. After he's gone, you're going to be looking for a replacement, right? No, don't look at me. Just touch your nose with your left hand for a yes."

Don said, "I've got a school to run here. Somebody better do something and it had better be quick."

Jamie opened the bag with his free hand. He grasped the bottom seam and turned the contents onto the table.

"For the love of Mike!" said Hank.

"I told you he was fried. I must see this kind of thing two, three times a week," said Bruno.

Kate said, "It can't be as bad as all this, Jamie. I realize that the job has its dreadful moments now and then, but come on."

"I stayed as long as I could – "

" – You've said enough, Kerwood."

"I STAYED AS LONG AS I COULD trying to keep the crows away. He looked peaceful with his head all tucked in like that, as if he were preparing for winter again. He had fought and fought, only to give up in the spring sun. I jumped and hooted and threw clods of dirt at the black birds dancing lazily out of the way. The sun came up a burning orange. The crows cocked their heads to one side, then the other."

"You know," said Don, "I did not need this today, people. I have a budget deadline to meet, curriculum meetings this afternoon, staffing meetings all this week. Your timing is impeccable, Kerwood. Somebody get one of the custodial staff in here. Kerwood, if you're still here when I come back in five minutes, I'll have you arrested."

As they walked out of the staff room, Bruno said to Hank,

"I know how this kind of thing works. I've been around. All I'm saying is we go through the regular channels, the 'pee-pee' list and all that, but somehow, mysteriously, my résumé keeps floating to the top of the list. Do you understand what I'm saying to you, Hank? It's the way the world works. You know me, I know you. Are you listening? I'm the guy who can walk into the middle of Jacko's darlings without a prep and emerge unscathed. You should have seen me in there. I was magnificent. I'm someone you can count on."

"Not like him," said Hank with a note of uncertainty.

"Not like him. That's for sure. So, what do you say? It sure would be nice to go home tonight to the wife with some good news. Do you think you can see your way clear? Hank?"

Only Jamie and Susan were left. She stood.

"I think he means it."

"You go," he said.

"Why? There's nothing here for you anymore. They don't want you."

"I'm tired. I just need time to think."

Gingerly, Susan slipped the feathered head into the muddied bag.

day of reckoning

Two security guards flanking the Director of Human Resources arrived at Martin's office at five minutes past ten in the morning. The Director was an aloof, professional woman with whom Martin had had only passing contact since their introduction two years before. She and the two male officers walked in, unannounced by prim but flustered James. The woman spoke in an even, slightly tremulous alto, shaky, Martin hoped, because of the disagreeable nature of her task.

"Mr. Kingdom," she said, "please accompany these officers out of the building. You are kindly asked to take nothing with you and to speak to no one on your way out."

He was allowed to put on his winter coat and his overshoes. On his way down the hall to the elevator he tried to meet, in a reassuring way, the searching eyes of his colleagues and staff. There was no trying to make light of it. He surrendered his keys. Access codes to his computer files would be changed if they had not already been. Poor, bird-like James would be reassigned. It was an even bet that Martin had been the last to know.

Although you might share an elevator with Martin Kingdom without being duly impressed by him one way or the other, having no way of knowing from his broad face and rounded body if he was one of the powerful, you probably know the product for which he was responsible. You may even be one of millions who consume it. The television commercials which strive to make the product attractive by dint of its quirky unconventionality – his. He had commissioned each one. He was often to be seen on the production set. At its apogee, in and around his camp, his success erected a canny informality born of imperial confidence.

But now is a time of shrouded, graceless formality when doubt and paucity of vision advise commerce, government, and the family. Martin knew that this time, this decline that was not only his but his product's, his firm's, his country's, was coming. He had been one of the first to whisper it knowingly in the company suites, even as he was arranging the unlikely marriages that so distinguished the image of his product: Supreme Court justices tutored in the finer points of jurisprudence by preschool tots, teenage grunge rockers crooning to honey-toned easy-listening love songs, senior citizens bungee-jumping off notable landmarks. His studied brand of frivolity would soon be out of favour. For is it not true that as hope dwindles with savings we no longer believe we can afford frivolity?

Reviewing it the way an athlete obsesses over a losing performance – a rimmed putt, a stranded rock, an imperfect lean at the tape – he fingered the possible reasons for his decline. The easiest, least hurtful, and least true, would have said something about the state of the economy. Months earlier, even as he phoned his secretary from home with an excuse of a Monday mid-morning, or apologized to his team for missing an important monthly strategy session, or depended overly much on the zeal of his junior associates, he knew that his day, this day of reckoning, was fast approaching. He was being sacrificed, he knew that much, but why? Had it been a single transgression that had turned them against him, or many?

There were preconditions. The report linking a certain additive in the product to health problems, it should be noted, was one of the first files passed to him when he took his position, and a lawsuit, a class action that named not only the company but many of its executive employees including Martin, was five years old, now as institutionalized and mythical as *Jarndyce and Jarndyce* itself. They referred to it only as The Case. But he kept returning to the change in himself, the softening of focus, the hint of intolerance. He had pushed away months before everyone else. Certainly none of the focus-group leaders or market pollsters or intuitive crystal-ball-gazers could detect it. What of the edifice of images, words, store shelves, factories, lives? Could one person alone topple it?

* * *

His neighbours, two fit middle-aged women, husbands of substantial means, houses in good standing on the nicest street, Martin's street, in the safest neighbourhood of the city, had bought identical wolfhounds and were walking them together that Monday morning through the wooded park. One of the women, whom he recognized, always remembered Martin's name.

"Snatching a bit of the R and R this morning, are we, Martin?" she said.

"Hello there, how are you?" he said. "Yes, beautiful day. Couldn't resist getting out in it."

"How is Melinda?"

"Fine," he said, "just fine."

"Please give her my love, Martin. Tell her I'll call."

"Oh, I will. You bet..."

"Vivian."

"Vivian. Yes. Well, goodbye."

They parted at the park gates. In a clear patch of ground off to one side of the parking lot, a man was pitching horseshoes. Martin had seen the little man before in the summer playing a board game or croquet by himself and had always dismissed him as simpleton. He had the gangly, match stick body of an eleven-year-old but the toothless, wrinkled face of an old man. Martin sat down on a nearby bench to watch.

The horseshoes were a child's set made of coloured plastic, red and blue, and the stakes at either end of the pitch were twigs held upright in a cairn of stones. The player tossed four red horseshoes, strode across the pitch to survey the result, mumbled to himself as if calculating and storing the score, and then turned to throw the blue set. Because there were only three of this colour, the man deliberated for an instant, stooped to retrieve the one furthest from the stake, walked back across the pitch, and threw again. This last one ringed the stick and stayed, and the man giggled.

It occurred to Martin, as the match progressed, that two distinct personalities were emerging in the little man. When he turned to throw the red horseshoes, his back and shoulders stiffened and he set his face in a grim pout. After each toss, he dropped his head and shook it from side to side, grumbling to himself, even if the shoe landed close to the target. Martin could not distinguish words as he watched the thin lips move, but imagined the man speaking the way a nagging parent might to a lazy child. The player kicked the toe of his sneaker into the hard ground. Reluctantly, it seemed, he shuffled forward to see how he had done.

As the blue player, he could hardly stand still as he prepared his throws. Little ripples of excitement played up and down his now loose, animated body. After every attempt, unable to wait until the end of the set, he would skip towards the stake for a closer look. He returned, held the toy close to his chest with both hands, closed his eyes and tilted his head skyward. All the while a tinny instrumental polka played on an old, battery-run tape recorder sitting on the ground beside his knapsack.

The sun disappeared behind a cloud, and Martin began to shiver. He stood up. It would be time for lunch soon and Melinda would be looking for him. He hoped that it would be something simple today, not vichyssoise or borscht or bouillabaisse but a creamy tomato from a can, and a grilled cheddar on brown bread, tastes from his childhood. Those winter days after rioting for morning hours in snow, being told to stand still as his mother stripped him of frost-encrusted layers, seeing his hair in the mirror bristle with static electricity, gulping the too-hot soup which he chased with cold milk.

"Hello," he said, but the man did not reply. Martin took a few steps forward and called again, "Would you mind if I threw a couple?"

The man froze, a red horseshoe held to his lips. He did not turn his head to look at Martin but remained standing there in profile.

"Play you a game," said Martin, the way he remembered saying it when he was a boy, that suggestion as natural as breath and sleep.

The man let out a high little whine and turned his shoulders inward, away from the intruder. He paused, bowed like that, then made a dash for his bag. The music snapped off, the horseshoes disappeared into the knapsack along with the tape player, and the man hustled away down a path into the woods, leaving only his makeshift stakes behind.

When he arrived home, Martin noted with some relief that he was only a few minutes later than usual. He called hello but got no answer. The kitchen was empty, the table unset. A new amaryllis, its blossom still sheathed in green, its pot wrapped in shiny red foil, sat in the sink. He went upstairs where he found Melinda lying on the bed.

She said, "Vivian Oberlander said she saw you in the park in the middle of the morning. She called me right away and I called James. "Isn't he home yet?" James said and I said, "No, why should he be?" and he said, "Then he hasn't told you yet?" "Told me what?" I said....Oh, Martin, what are we going to do?"

"You shouldn't worry," he said. "This is not the end of the world."

"They sent me a lily. By courier. Did you see it? They send lilies to mourners, Martin. Mourners," and the tears, not new from the look of the balled tissues strewn about the coverlet, came in a torrent.

Later, when she was ready, he assured Melinda that the severance payment would amply meet their needs, for a whole year if necessary. Martin Kingdom was well known in the industry. He was a free agent. People would soon be calling with offers. He almost wished the telephone not ring just yet, so that he and she might have some time together.

"We'll go away," he said. "Somewhere warm and ancient. When was the last time we had the luxury of doing something like that?"

The severance papers and his belongings, the grandfather clock, the paintings, the photographs, all the contents of his desk that were not company property, and the rosewood desk itself, came the next day by special delivery. All was accounted for, wrapped carefully, probably mournfully by James who included in the center drawer a note of deep regret written in his calligrapher's script on lavender-scented vellum.

Martin signed the manifest and tipped the two grateful delivery men ten dollars apiece. In an envelope marked "Personal & Confidential" was the letter of termination thanking him for his "many years of service to the company," his "outstanding contributions to the financial health of the firm," his "never-to-be-forgotten legacy" as a mentor and team leader able to "inspire a generation of young, fertile minds." With the letter, signed by his superior, the vice-president of sales and marketing, a bloodless man he used to joke about behind his back, was a cheque made out to Martin for just over two months' salary. He turned the letter over in his hands, looked again inside the large manila envelope, turned it upside down and shook it, but nothing more emerged.

Before he dialled, he decided to be restrained and conciliatory. He had to be content with leaving a message. When the vice-president phoned back an hour later, Martin said,

"You might have dispensed with the dramatics."

"You know the routine, Martin. It's nothing personal."

The man went on to explain that the change in policy regarding the size of the severance payment had been made on the advice of the accounting department. In light of the trend in the industry towards streamlining and downsizing, greater efficiency and trimmer budgets, the termination package had been made standard for all employees at two and one-quarter month's salary.

"How am I supposed to live on that?"

"You must have investment income, Martin."

"That's beside the point. I originated that package. It's got my name all over it. You can't tell me now that I'm not entitled to what we all agreed upon. I'll sue."

The calm voice reminded him that the company could afford a battery of lawyers. Just how many could he afford right now?

"I assumed I needed only one."

But there would be no winning, he knew. The company had offices and distribution outlets on every continent except Antarctica, in every city of a hundred thousand or more. If it were allowed, and if it deigned to do so, it could claim a seat at the United Nations. Fighting the company would be like trying to drink the ocean.

"I don't think you're in any position to be suing anyone at the moment, old man."

"Meaning?"

"The Case. Rumour has it we're pretty close to a settlement on it."

"I am covered under the company plan, am I not? For the time I was employed."

"Technically, yes."

"Expand on that point, Bob, if you would, please."

"I'm sorry. I really can't say anything more."

He knew it! They were offering him up as a sacrificial lamb. They were saying, "See, here is the culprit. You will notice that we have since fired him. He knew about the health risks in the product and still he continued to promote it. Yes, the company takes full responsibility for the safety of its product, but if individuals must be named...well...one need look no further than

Martin Kingdom. Just look at the images he brought to the screen. Are they not deceptive? Did they did not contribute in a substantial way to this tragic event?"

Martin had made more money for them in the past decade than anyone else. Two months' measly salary! Personal liability! He had given the company most of his adult life. He owned some preferred company shares whose dividends paid modestly. He and Melinda could live on that, he supposed, as long as the market remained vital. They might have to move to a smaller house, reduce their monthly expenses, but it could be done. They were not destitute. Far from it. And the phone would soon be ringing. But the indignity of it.

On the weekend the telephone did ring. Their son, Anthony called from college to inquire, politely, reservedly, after his father's well-being. The boy had heard about the sacking from a friend. Martin assured him that there was nothing to worry about.

"You might have to take a part-time job, Tony, just for a while, just for pocket change. They must have things like that on campus, at the book store or the pub. Don't tell your mother this, but the old man didn't get quite the golden handshake he was expecting."

"Dad, I've been thinking maybe I should come home, help out a bit, you know. Maybe get a job there. I could pick up again where I left off next semester."

"Don't you think about it, boy. No way. You keep hitting those books and don't you get sidetracked. You hear me? Everything is all right here. You're covered."

In the middle of the week the market fell sharply for the third consecutive day and Martin cashed his company stock. He sent Tony enough to pay his tuition and his living expenses for the remainder of the term and put the rest in Melinda's savings account. On the walk home, he felt in control. True, there had been no offers of employment yet, but he was sure they were coming. True, what should have been a year's cushion was three or four months' at best, but he was healthy and resourceful, at

114

the peak of his powers. He strode along the wide boulevard, a confident man, enjoying being outside and pulling into his lungs this bright, best part of the day.

It became his routine to linger with Melinda over breakfast and coffee in the morning, returning occasionally afterward to bed. The hour or two before noon he then spent either talking on the telephone, leaving messages and setting up meetings, or fine-tuning his résumé. Most of his interviews he scheduled over lunch, at expensive restaurants where he had been accustomed to entertaining and being entertained at the company's expense, and he made it a point of honour to continue picking up the cheque. Around four o'clock he would return home, often gloomy, bordering on drunk, sometimes to join Melinda for a sobering tea, but increasingly to an empty house and a note indicating her plans with this or that friend for the evening. He would then sleep until early evening, when he would wake, eat a light meal in front of the television set, and doze again until she came home, often at one or two o'clock in the morning.

She left him in the spring, after the lawsuit was finally settled. Hardly a surprise to him, Martin was one of only a few found liable in the case. He was compelled to sell the house, the cars, and furniture to pay his legal fees and the sixty percent of the award not covered by his insurance. Melinda moved in with her sister and brother-in-law in another city. Anthony took up residence with his girl friend and her parents, and Martin found an apartment overlooking the park.

For months a combative spirit remained alive in him and he continued to beg Melinda to come back. They had been young and penniless and in love once, did she not remember? He described his little rooms to her. Weren't they exactly like that first apartment they had rented just before Anthony was born? Where was the young, spirited woman he had fallen in love with, the one who had said that she needed nothing, not food or clothing or shelter, but his kiss alone to sustain her? It was not fair to pin her down in that far-off moment, she said. They had grown together and as individuals, she said. She wasn't a young woman any more. She had expectations in this life.

"Grow with me again," he said. "I can do anything as long as it is with you. Please." He said this on the telephone, at all times of the day and night, when he was drunk and maudlin and when he was sober and logical.

When her sister changed the number and ceased to list it, he travelled the three hours by bus to see his wife. Jerry, the husband, a man Martin almost never thought about, came outside to talk some sense.

"I'm not going to let you in the house, Marty, because nothing good will come of it, and I'm sure-as-shooting not going to let you make a scene for the neighbours by raising your voice out here on the front steps. So why don't you just let me take you over to the motel. We can get a drink there and you can get a room for the night. My treat. Let me do that much for you. You've helped Darlene and me out plenty in the past. You've taken some real body blows lately. I can only imagine what you're going through. But believe me, nothing good will come of harassing Melinda. She's not ready to see you yet."

He let Jerry take his suitcase from him and lead him to the car. A whole river drained from him, conquering intention reduced to silt. He said he would skip the drink, if it was all the same to Jerry. He apologized for causing trouble. Jerry, in a way that sounded less kindly than it might have under other conditions, told him not to say anything more about it.

In the morning he drove Martin to the bus station and passed him a folded hundred dollar bill when they shook hands goodbye. Martin looked at it in his hand. Jerry strode away before Martin could offer the polite show of refusal convention required.

* * *

He passed the summer and fall sitting at his window looking out at the entrance to the park, venturing out only to the grocery store and the bank. It seemed that every time he went to the bank he made some mistake, whether it was filling out the amount of his withdrawal on a deposit form, or forgetting to sign it, or getting the date wrong. One day the teller did not catch that he had put the wrong amount down on his deposit slip until after she had made the entry in the computer. Martin began to fill out a new deposit slip and became confused when the teller asked him simply to initial her changes to his original: a new total, a different amount deducted in cash, and the same net deposit.

"Why can't I just make out a new one?" he said.

"It's already in the system," she said. She had red hair and a patient, knowing smile.

"Listen, I don't want all that change rattling around in my pocket. Ninety-three cents? I want an even number to carry away, dollars, no cents."

"Sir, it's not my fault that you put the wrong amount down."

"Yes, I understand that. I don't care what the deposit is, really, as long as it's in the general ball park. What I don't want to have to contend with is all this silver. I sit down somewhere, I lose it."

"Why don't you deposit the ninety-three cents back into your account?" she suggested. "That will leave you with an even ninety-four dollars."

"Because I need to have a hundred." He made up a story on the spot. "I have to buy my son a pair of basketball shoes. Have you seen the price of basketball shoes lately? He won't make do with anything less, of course. They inflate once he puts them on. Does this...make any...?"

"All right, sir. Why don't we do this? Why don't you deposit the ninety-three cents back in and withdraw another six dollars? That will give you an even hundred."

Martin thought about what she had said. It made sense. For the first time he noticed her name tag: Colleen O'Brien. Just how Irish was she? He wanted to reach across the counter to touch her hair. What would make her lose her patience?

"The bank charges me every time I make a transaction, doesn't it?"

"Yes, that is correct, sir, thirty-five cents."

"What you're telling me, then, is that if I do all the things you're telling me to do, three transactions in all, you'll debit my account – what is it now?" and he began to add the numbers in the air in front of him.

"Dollar five," said Colleen O'Brien.

"One dollar and five cents. I will lose money because I would rather withdraw an even sum of money. My money. Mine. Does that make any sense to you? It makes precious little sense to me."

"May I ask you something, sir? Why would a man who is willing to throw a hundred dollars down on a pair of running shoes, that his son will either destroy or grow out of in six months, quibble about a dollar and five cents?"

* * *

Every day that it was not raining, the little man arrived to stake out his territory, either in the grassy clearing where Martin had seen him playing horseshoes that day or upon the granite base of a statue where he spread out his board games and listened to his music. Martin thought that the figure of the statue, a World War I soldier, resembled the child-man beneath it. Remembering how he had frightened him away, Martin was content to watch from a distance like an unseen guardian.

* * *

Just before his money ran out, Martin got temporary work with the post office delivering Christmas mail. It got him outside, walking again, and eating regularly. Because he had no vehicle, he spent most of each day, for most of the month of December, on buses and on foot, and when he returned to his two little rooms he felt weary, worked clean, and peaceful. He liked breathing the cold air and seeing the look on people's faces when he handed them a big parcel wrapped in brown paper with the words, "DO NOT OPEN UNTIL CHRIST-MAS" emblazoned across it. Once he called at the home of his and Melinda's former neighbour, Vivian Oberlander, but the woman did not recognize him in his blue post office jacket and new beard. She insisted that he wait while she rooted through her purse for a tip. Sometimes he had to stand for a long time in apartment building entrances before anyone would let him in and sometimes the people who answered their doors were suspicious or angry or indifferent, but for most he was like Santa Claus and it made him happy.

His wife and son telephoned on Christmas morning. Melinda asked if he had found a position yet and he told her he had, that it was not in the same field but a related one, distribution. She said that that was good, she was glad for him. She said that Darlene and Jerry were being awfully nice putting her up and helping her find a place of her own. She had been offered a job with the same manufacturing company she had been working for when she and Martin had met. It was not down on the floor this time but over at head office as their Special Events and Travel Coordinator. He congratulated her. She sounded to him like a nineteen-year-old again, brave, loud, tripping over words left behind by her thoughts.

"I never dreamed that they would pay me– Martin, you won't believe what my starting salary is. Go ahead, guess. No, don't, it's embarrassing. What was I saying? Oh, yes, that they would pay me to plan dinner parties and galas and getaway weekends in places like Aruba? It's the kind of thing I was born to do. Oh, but I'm blathering. Tony's here. He's staying for the holidays. Did I say Merry Christmas, Martin? Merry Christmas, darling. I do hope you're well. It's all worked out for the best, hasn't it? Tell me that you think it has."

He said yes, he believed it had. He asked her when he could see her again, but the phone on her end had already been put down and he could hear her calling for Tony. Martin felt his heart begin to race and his palms become clammy. He had nothing to say to his son, no wisdom, no assurance, no answers to the hard questions: Why hadn't Martin tried harder? Why couldn't he and Melinda see that they needed each other, that they were better together than apart? Why had they not considered their son's feelings and needs?

Whenever Anthony had called in the past and Martin had answered, he had always been able to pass the phone quickly to Melinda or, if she had not been home, at least tell his son to save his money and let her call him back. It was not that he did not love the boy. He just assumed that he would want to speak to his mother more than to him, that if the boy needed bolstering emotionally then she was better suited to that sort of thing. For Martin, the telephone was a business tool, used to fashion transactions and construct new relationships. If there was a problem, you did something to solve it. You talked in order to establish the parameters of a situation and then you agreed on the best course of action and then you acted. Anything more just tended to complicate matters unduly. This speaking for the sake of hearing a loved one's voice, this he felt was best left to others.

He returned the receiver to its cradle before Tony came on the line, and sat in his chair by the window. The massed wishes of the city had made it snow in the night, a downy comforter dressing the trees and the rooftops and the helmet of the unknown soldier in holy white. The crazy little guy was sitting on his regular spot on the statue's pedestal, catching snowflakes on his tongue. The woman who ran the corner store came out holding a lidded styrofoam cup. He took a sip and immediately, tongue out, head shaking back and forth, handed the cup back to her. She scooped some snow off the statue and put it on his tongue, laughing lovingly.

Martin bathed and shaved and went across the street to a lunch counter where he treated himself to a fried egg, toast, sausages and coffee for breakfast. He bought a newspaper on his way out and brought it back to the apartment. The phone was ringing when he got in and he hesitated before reaching for it. If it was Anthony, he thought, what was the harm in speaking with his son on a Christmas morning? If the boy was angry, then he had a right to it. Martin had weathered worse. After the boy had vented, his father would simply say that he was sorry, that he never meant to hurt anyone, that he'd thought about it and still didn't know what he'd done wrong.

Sometimes bad things happen to people, Tony, and there's not much they can do except persevere. I'd like it if we could get together soon and spend some time. You could let me know how you're doing, what your plans are. It's a sure bet you're in love and thinking about getting married. We could talk about that, not that I can give you any fast and true answers, only my observations. Maybe if I'd had a chance to talk to my father about things like that....'

He picked up in mid-ring and said, "Listen, Tony, I'm sorry I– "

"No, Martin, it's Cal at the main depot. Wasn't sure if I'd be able to get you. I was wondering if you're available to make some deliveries today. Double time and a half."

"Oh, I'm– I really don't know, Cal. Christmas Day."

"That's perfectly all right. I understand. I'll see if I can get somebody else. I just thought that since you're alone there and everything...."

"Wait," said Martin, "on second thought, what the heck. I could use the exercise."

"That's the lad! It's a big load. You'll have a truck today. It'll be ready when you get here."

The bus he had to take stopped right beside the entrance to the park and he went outside to wait in the glassed-in shelter. The little man was still sitting under the soldier and now he had his board game unfolded beside him. The lightly falling snow covered the board, and every turn or two he carefully blew the flakes away.

Martin watched him play for a while and then stuck his head out of the bus shelter.

"How are you doing?" he said, fully expecting the man to pack up and run away again.

"All right," he said, not looking up from the game.

* * *

Martin missed two passes of his bus and did not finish his mail deliveries until late in the afternoon, the last few stops interrupting some turkey dinners, but no one was annoyed and some invited him in for egg nog. One man insisted that he knew Martin from somewhere, but Martin only smiled and was of no help. He kept thinking about the little man, who had won the game, sitting beneath the statue of the Unknown Soldier, catching snowflakes on his tongue.

Richard Cumyn grew up in Ottawa, and was educated at Queen's University. He is the author of *The Limit of Delta Y Over Delta X*. His stories have appeared widely in magazines and have been anthologized in *Under NeWest Eyes*, *The Journey Prize Anthology*, *Stag Line*, and *The Grand-Slam Book of Canadian Baseball Writing*. He lives in Kingston, Ontario.